Bello:

hidden talent rediscovered!

Bello is a digital only imprint of Pan Macmillan, established to breathe new life into previously published, classic books.

At Bello we believe in the timeless power of the imagination, of good story, narrative and entertainment and we want to use digital technology to ensure that many more readers can enjoy these books into the future.

We publish in ebook and Print on Demand formats to bring these wonderful books to new audiences.

About Bello:

www.panmacmillan.com/imprints/bello

About the author:

www.panmacmillan.com/author/rcsherriff

R. C. Sherriff

On his return from the First World War, R. C. Sherriff settled in London, working as an insurance agent and writing plays in the evening. *Journey's End*, inspired by Sherriff's own experience of fighting, was his sixth play but the first to be given a professional production. It was an immediate, outstanding and phenomenal success. Thirty-one separate productions ran concurrently around the world and it was translated into twenty six languages. Its success, however, was both a boon and a burden – while it allowed him to give up the day job and devote himself full-time to writing, it often overshadowed his later work or was used as the yardstick against which it was measured unfavourably.

Fortunately for Sherriff he was not only a playwright but also a novelist and a screenwriter. He wrote a bestselling novel, *A Fortnight In September* in 1931, and the screenplays for *The Invisible Man* (1933), *The Four Feathers* (1939) and classic films such as *Goodbye Mr Chips* (1939), for which he received an Oscar nomination, and *The Dambusters* (1955).

Although Sherriff was occupied as a playwright and screenwriter he did not lose his urge to write novels and he followed the success of his first novel with *The Hopkins Manuscript*, *Chedworth*, *Another Year* and others. Now, while *Journey's End* continues to define Sherriff's reputation, much of his work remains ripe for rediscovery.

R. C. Sherriff

THE SEIGE OF SWAYNE CASTLE

BELLO

First published in 1973 by Gollancz

This edition published 2012 by Bello
an imprint of Pan Macmillan, a division of Macmillan Publishers Limited
Pan Macmillan, 20 New Wharf Road, London N1 9RR
Basingstoke and Oxford
Associated companies throughout the world

www.panmacmillan.com/imprints/bello
www.curtisbrown.co.uk

ISBN 978-1-4472-2106-7 EPUB
ISBN 978-1-4472-2105-0 POD

A CIP catalogue record for this book is available from the British Library.

Chapter One

All day the woodlands around the castle had echoed to the thud of axes and the crash of falling trees.

Fires were blazing where brushwood had been piled; wagons loaded with timber had made ceaseless journeys to the castle, stacking the trunks behind the ramparts for winter fuel.

Beyond the woodlands they were scything the green corn. In a few weeks it would have made a fine harvest. It was useless now except as fodder for the cattle to be kept in the enclosure behind the walls.

Hogs had been slaughtered, the meat dried and salted and stored in the vaults. The skins had been dressed and set aside for warmth if bitter weather came. The marshes had been scoured for the hard-stemmed reeds used for arrow shafts. From the nearby beach had come the smooth round stones for the catapults.

Away in the distance they could see dust clouds rising from the slow advancing army. It would be a long and pitiless siege. Lord Swayne and his men had no delusions about that. The Earl had sworn to smash the castle to the ground; to hang the garrison amidst its ruins and wipe the pestilent Swaynes off the face of the earth.

Lord Swayne had returned the compliment by declaring that the Earl, with all his massive strength, would never take the castle: not if he beat his head against its walls until the crack of doom.

For the sake of his men he had to fling defiance in good measure, but he was too realistic for wishful thinking. When it came to open conflict with the Earl it was David against Goliath, and he knew it.

He had no personal quarrel with the Earl. The seeds were planted years before, when Duke William of Normandy had come with his invading army and the Island had fallen into his hands like a ripe plum.

The Conqueror had less to fear from the defeated English than from his own Norman barons who had pledged their support in return for English plunder. He had to reward them with large estates without making them over-powerful.

His most dangerous supporter had been Count Godfrey of Valmont. His contribution had been a massive one. Apart from a large contingent of mounted men he had supplied seven ships. In return he had received a fine estate in East Anglia, but it was landlocked, and for his own special reasons Count Godfrey wanted an outlet to the sea.

A few miles from the Count's estate was a harbour and a stretch of sea coast that would suit him perfectly. It was in the hands of a small settlement of English called the Swaynes: farmers and fishermen who had built themselves a town and a few fishing villages along the coast. They were peaceful people who only wanted to be left alone.

Count Godfrey asked the Conqueror to grant him this small property. Now that the invasion was successfully completed he wanted his seven ships back.

'I can keep them in that harbour,' he explained. 'From there it will be an easy journey to my estates in Normandy, and I can go to and fro whenever I find it necessary.'

He wanted the harbour badly, but the Conqueror wasn't fool enough to let him have it. Count Godfrey had powerful friends in the Low Countries hostile to Duke William. The harbour would be an open door to any mischief that he contemplated. In alliance with his friends he could plan a new invasion. With the harbour as a beach-head he could build up a massive army to conquer the Island for himself.

The Conqueror accordingly told the Count that he had decided to make the Swayne property a Royal domain. The Count, he said, could keep his seven ships at Dover and sail from there whenever he wanted to visit his estates in Normandy. This was safe enough because Dover was securely under Royal control.

Count Godfrey was beside himself with rage and indignation. To allow this splendid harbour to remain in the hands of despised, defeated 'natives' was an insult to a Norman aristocrat, but there was nothing he could do about it. To take a Royal domain by force would be rebellion, and Count Godfrey, by himself, could not risk a conflict with his powerful master.

It left a wound that festered through the years. Hatred for the Swaynes became an obsession with the Valmont family. Passed on from father to son was the conviction that the Swayne property was theirs by right: but they had been cheated out of it by the Conqueror.

They were powerless so long as the Crown was strong enough to protect its Royal domain, but they bided their time. One day the chance would come, and they would use it without mercy.

It came at last when John was King, when the Island was torn by civil war: some barons for the King, some against.

The Valmont family was now an Earldom, and the head of it was a crafty man. He had sided with the King, and saw a heaven-sent chance to get hold of the Swayne property.

The barons hostile to the King had given the Earl a hand of trumps when they had offered the English crown to the son of the King of France. He went to King John and played his cards with excellent results.

'We all know,' he said, 'that your enemies have offered your crown to the French Dauphin who is preparing a strong army to invade. Dover and the south coast are secure, but there is a harbour on the east coast open to invasion with a castle in the hands of one of your enemies. Lord Swayne is dangerous. He has made no declaration of loyalty to you in your present troubles. On the contrary he has talked openly of his sympathy with those who want to overthrow you. A word from them, and he will throw his harbour and castle wide open to the French.

'We must act quickly. The Swaynes themselves are a small community but they have the means to give your enemies everything they need. I have the resources to prevent it. If you give me a Royal warrant, I will soon hold that harbour and castle securely in your name.'

King John was grateful to the Earl for drawing his attention to this wide-open door for a French invasion and he welcomed having it firmly shut by such a stalwart and dependable loyalist.

'Very well, my good friend,' he said. 'Take the castle and the harbour and hold them safely for the Crown. When my present troubles are over you may rest assured that your services will not go unrewarded.'

And he gave the Earl the warrant that he needed.

The Earl was delighted. He had got the best of both worlds. To have taken the Swayne territory under cover of a civil war was to risk being called to account when peace returned: when the re-established King, or future King, would want to know by what authority he had invaded a Royal domain.

But a Royal warrant covered everything. He could wipe out the Swaynes and take their castle by Royal command, and the King's promise that his services 'would not go unrewarded' could surely mean that the Swayne territory would be his for the asking.

There was another asset in that priceless warrant.

By feudal law the tenants of a great baron were obliged to give military service for a specified period each year. This usually meant their support in 'private wars', baron against baron, but tenants disliked getting mixed up in family feuds that didn't concern them. If a baron could collect half his retainers he was lucky and even those would be half-hearted.

But it was different when their overlord produced a warrant to conduct a campaign by order of the King himself. Refusal to serve the King was mutiny, and the Earl lost no time in sending copies of the warrant to every important tenant on his wide estates.

He made it plain that the campaign would be a short and victorious one, and hinted at valuable rewards. The Swayne settlement would be broken up and everything worth having would be divided among his men as spoils of war.

His retainers needed no further inducement, and the meadows

around the Earl's castle began to assume the appearance of a great armed camp.

Lord Swayne soon got to know what was going on.

It came as no surprise to him. For a long time he had seen that Royal power crumbling. He knew that the day was not far off when his people would have to face this onslaught. His first impulse had been to go to the King and tell him that he was no traitor: that as custodian of a Royal domain he would gladly hold the castle with all his power against a foreign invasion. But he knew that the Earl had poisoned the King's mind against him. The suspicious King would clap him into prison and leave the Earl to take his land without resistance.

The only course was to fight it out, with little enough to pin his hopes on. They were a small community, without the equipment or the manpower toface the Earl in open warfare. He staked his chances on the castle built by Henry Plantagenet to protect the harbour from invasion. It was a solid, stone-built, moated fortress on open land; as good for defence against the Earl as for its original purpose against invasion from the sea.

He chose forty of his best men for its garrison.

There was the problem of the older people and children who lived in the town. It was customary, in a mediaeval siege, for an honourable assailant to leave the civilians alone and concentrate upon the castle. But Swayne put no trust in the Earl's good faith, and arranged to evacuate his people to the outlying farms and fishing villages.

He had to think more carefully about his own family: his wife and daughter, and Roger his son. If the Earl could lay hands on them he would make good use of them as hostages – if in fact he allowed them to survive. Swayne had arranged to send them to the safety of a monastery near Norwich. Not even the Earl would dare to violate a sanctuary, but his son had flatly refused to go.

Roger was fourteen, tall and strong for his age, and had begged his father to let him remain as one of the castle garrison. For a long time Swayne had insisted that Roger should go. He had no delusions about the Earl's main purpose. He wanted the Swayne property and would only achieve half his purpose if he killed Swayne but failed to kill his heir as well. The laws of inheritance were strictly enforced. King John might grant the property to the Earl, but if an heir remained, and came of age, there was every chance of his regaining the property from a future King.

He tried to explain this to his son, but Roger dug his heels in.

'I won't go!' he declared. 'If you tied me up and sent me to that monastery by force, I'd escape and come back here!'

Swayne stood firm, but he was breaking the boy's heart.

'There's lots I can do,' Roger said. 'Carry messages, clean weapons, stand guard with the men, take duty on the watch tower. When it comes to a fight I can draw a bow as strongly as any of the men. And what's more, I know the castle better than anybody – I could find my way around it blindfold.'

On that he was no doubt right. Since his earliest boyhood he had been leader of a small gang of boys who had held the deserted castle against all manner of ferocious imaginary enemies. They had manned the ramparts, shouted orders through the dark empty corridors of the keep and made fierce sorties across the drawbridge. Roger loved the castle; to him it was a fortress of enchantment, and now that it was to be defended in reality, nothing on God's earth would make him leave it.

Swayne finally gave way. He knew the deadly risk. How delighted the Earl would be when he heard that he had both Swayne and his only son cornered in the castle! Against this he measured the harm it would do Roger: the shame and humiliation of being shut up for safety in a monastery while the garrison was fighting for the castle.

So one night he called Roger to him and said, 'I've decided to let you be one of the garrison. There'll be hard work for you, and I'm trusting you to do it well.'

And Roger went to bed in a seventh heaven.

Chapter Two

The Earl was a bulky man beyond the usual age for riding out to war, but two good reasons urged him on. The first, of course, was the conquest of a fine coastal property that his family had wanted for years. His second was to prove himself a warrior. He had always longed for military renown, but so far his ambitions had been unfulfilled.

As a young man he had fought under King Richard in the Holy Land. He was proud to call himself a Crusader: never tired of talking about his exploits. But the other Barons, who knew the facts, said it was nothing but hot air. Whenever King Richard had ordered an assault, they said, the Earl had succumbed to an acute attack of fever which laid him low until the assault was over.

These stories stuck. He had never had a chance to redeem himself, but now at last he could show what he was made of. The Swaynes were not a powerful enemy, but they had a castle, and castles were notoriously difficult to capture by assault. Usually the besiegers sat down outside and starved the garrison out, but that wasn't the Earl's idea at all. He would show the military world that a castle could be cracked open and destroyed like a nut beneath a hammer. It would be a spectacular assault with siege weapons of his own creation: a classic campaign, perfectly organized and carried out with immaculate precision. Above all it would silence the critics who called him a fatuous windbag.

His tenants, attracted by the promise of a short campaign with a bountiful share of loot, were providing men in gratifying numbers. The levies they brought in were amateur soldiers, mainly workers in the fields, useful for little more than guard duties and work around the camp. For his 'shock troops', the spearhead of the assault, he was depending upon professionals: mercenary soldiers who hired themselves out to any magnate who could afford to pay them.

In those days, when wars were nearly always going on, it was good business for an enterprising young man to raise his own Company. There was a young Captain named Raymond of Bethune who was known on the Continent as a skilled and courageous leader. The Earl, who was a wealthy man determined to hire the best, sent word to Raymond: offering to engage him with three hundred men for a guaranteed two months – ample time, he reckoned, to prepare the campaign and capture Swayne Castle.

Raymond was free. The money was good, so he enrolled his men, took ship for England, and reported to the Earl for duty.

Things didn't turn out as smoothly as the Earl expected. Had he hired a second-rate bunch of unemployed soldiers in England he could have made them do exactly what he wanted, but he had engaged the best young mercenary Captain in Europe, and Raymond soon made it clear that he expected to be given entire control of the campaign. This was the last thing that the Earl intended. He had cast himself for the leading role and wasn't going to sit back and let Raymond steal the thunder.

'I am by no means an inexperienced soldier,' he said, and went on to describe his exploits in the Holy Land. 'King Richard,' he said, 'employed siege weapons, but open to improvement. I am now constructing something of my own design that will be a revelation. In the hands of trained soldiers, under your control, it will be irresistible, and you, my dear Raymond, will gain great prestige as the soldier who first made use of it. But I must, of course, retain overall command.'

Raymond listened in silence. He was a handsome young man with a deep scar down one cheek and two fingers from his right hand missing. Vigour and command were written all over him. He had already summed up the Earl for what he was, but he had his own business to consider. The campaigning season on the Continent was over. He kept his best men together during the winter by paying them a retaining fee, and the Earl's money would come in very useful.

'I will agree to serve under your command,' he said, 'providing I am satisfied with this siege machine of yours. So first you must show it to me.'

The Earl was very pleased to show off his invention. 'I am having it constructed in strict secrecy,' he said. 'No word of it must reach the ears of our opponents. Even my own army will know nothing of it until it goes into action.'

He took Raymond to an inner courtyard of his castle, secluded behind high walls. A dozen carpenters and wheelwrights were working on some complicated instruments that on first sight had no connection with each other, but the Earl explained it all in detail: how the parts would be tooled and bolted together in a massive, overwhelming weapon.

'My plan,' he said, 'is to assemble it completely in this secret place, and for you to train your men in the use of it. We shall then dismantle it and pack it into wagons for the journey to Swayne Castle.'

Raymond didn't share the Earl's enthusiasm. The thing was too cumbersome for his liking, but he was not a hidebound soldier. Anything new appealed to him. The Earl's invention had points of interest, and he agreed to train his men to use it.

The Earl then took Raymond to the wide meadow beyond the castle where his army of retainers was encamped. He was doing things in style. The young recruits were being fitted out in leather tunics and green cloth caps embroidered with the Earl's insignia. Some were being trained in sword drill. Wagons were coming in, stacked with equipment. There were loads of arrows, dozens of iron lanterns, prefabricated timber huts, crossbows, cooking pots, stone missiles. In a field kitchen whole oxen were being roasted for the evening meal.

The castle and its surrounding meadows lay in a fertile valley between thickly wooded uplands. Concealed in the undergrowth lay three men, watching the activities below them. They took careful note of everything they saw, and at night took horse and galloped off into the darkness.

Swayne's men were busy preparing their old neglected castle to meet the storm.

The moat was dredged and widened. Loose stones in the ramparts were cemented in. Wall turrets were strengthened and the drawbridge was repaired and oiled. The ramparts enclosed five acres of pasture that would feed the livestock they took in. There would be no problem about fresh water. When King Henry had decided to build a castle here the site wasn't chosen until he had found a spring. When good water was found, a well was sunk, and the keep constructed to have the well beneath it in the vaults.

In a castle besieged the garrison needed men skilled in every sort of job, apart from its defence, and Swayne had chosen them not only for their bowmanship, but for their crafts. There were stonemasons to repair damaged walls; carpenters and cooks; a blacksmith to sharpen weapons and a man skilled in leatherwork to mend the shoes. There was a herdsman for the livestock and a butcher to slaughter the cattle when required; a baker for the bread; a man to keep the latrines in order and a tailor to repair torn clothes. It was a self-contained community in miniature.

One day something happened that delighted everybody but Swayne himself.

He was kept well informed of the Earl's preparations by the spies who watched from the surrounding woods, but there was always a risk that the Earl might send out a surprise raiding force.

To guard against this Swayne sent out every morning a reconnaissance party of half a dozen mounted men to patrol the boundaries of the Swayne territory and bring back news of anything suspicious going on in the Earl's domain across the border.

Roger was in this party. He was a good horseman and enjoyed an exhilarating gallop across the country on those fine summer days.

At one point a small river marked the boundary between the two estates. It was a good fishing river, and it had been the custom for the Earl's people to fish from their side of it and for Swayne's to fish from theirs.

One morning the reconnaissance party saw three men and a boy fishing from the side belonging to the Swaynes. At first they took them to be some of their own people from a nearby farm, but drawing nearer they saw to their indignation that the three men were in the green tunics worn by servants of the Earl's household.

Four horses were tethered on the far side of the river. A small boat was tied up near the fishermen, and it was clear what had been done and why. The Earl's side of the river was marshy and difficult to fish from, but the side belonging to the Swaynes was firm and easy.

It was the sort of insolence expected from the servants of the Earl. The horsemen were on the point of riding forward to order them off when Roger stopped them. He was bursting with suppressed excitement.

'Hold on!' he whispered. 'I know who that boy is.'

There was no doubt about it in Roger's mind. Two years ago King John had summoned a Royal Assembly at Norwich. All the great barons in those parts were called, together with tenants of Royal property, and Swayne had taken Roger with him. He would stand by the roadside as the great noblemen rode in with their retinues, and most magnificent of all was the Earl who now threatened to destroy them. He came with a large company of superbly mounted men and beside him rode a boy of about Roger's own age, finely attired in the dress of a young aristocrat.

'That is the Earl's son, Gregory,' said Roger's father.

Roger had never forgotten the proud, handsome boy. The Swaynes were workaday, unimportant people who came without display. Roger had envied Gregory from afar – and now, to his incredulous excitement, there was Gregory, calmly fishing with three attendants, on the Swayne's side of the river – in their power.

'If we can take him,' he whispered to his companions. 'What a prize it would be!'

In the concealment of the trees they quickly made their plans.

Roger and two others would gallop down to the moored boat to cut off a retreat. The others would do the rest.

It was all over in a minute. The fishermen were taken completely by surprise. They did not hear the galloping horses on the soft turf of the meadow until they were surrounded. The servants were so terrified that they put up no resistance, but the boy fought furiously. He was strong, and had no lack of courage. He drew the dagger from his belt and when it was wrenched away he fought like a demon with his fists until they bound him with a leather strap and lashed him to a horse.

The three servants begged piteously to be made captives too, dreading their fate when they faced the Earl with the awful news, but they were bundled into the boat and pushed out into midstream.

Swayne's people were jubilant when they heard the news. With such a prize in their hands they were well on the way to victory before the Earl had shot an arrow at them!

But Swayne saw things in a more realistic light.

'If you hadn't recognized the boy,' he said to Roger, 'he would have been sent across the river with the servants and good riddance to him.'

'But don't you want him!' exclaimed the astonished Roger.

Swayne shook his head. 'What am I to do with him? If I offer him back to the Earl on his pledge to abandon the siege it wouldn't mean a thing. Once he got his son back he would go ahead without a scruple. Some barons would threaten blackmail. They'd tell the Earl that if he dared attack their castle they'd mutilate the boy and put his eyes out. Would you like me to do that?'

'You know I wouldn't,' said Roger.

'Then what?' asked his father.

'Make the Earl pay ransom money.'

'Money wouldn't help us to defend the castle,' said Swayne. 'If I had my way I'd show our contempt for the Earl by sending his son back without a word. But our own people wouldn't understand a thing like that. In their eyes we've made a priceless capture. If I threw the prize away they'd think I had lost my wits.'

Roger was near to tears. He had expected his father's

commendation for a splendid capture, but all he had done was to add another burden to his father's load of cares.

'I'm sorry,' he said. 'At the time it seemed the only thing to do . . . the right thing . . . I'm sorry that it wasn't.'

Swayne took his son by the shoulders. 'There's nothing to blame yourself for, Roger. In your place I'd have done the same. When a man declares war on you and his son is fool enough to stray into your land, it's your job to take him and hold him captive. You did the right thing and you did it well. It's no fault of yours that the boy's a nuisance to us.'

He ordered that Gregory should be kept under guard in the house of Father Peter the priest until the siege began. He would then be taken as a captive to the castle.

There were soon more urgent things to cope with. A few nights later the spies rode in to report that all day there had been great activity in the Earl's encampment. The tents were being struck and loaded into wagons. A cavalcade of vehicles, stacked with equipment and weapons, had begun to assemble along the road, and the Earl himself, on a fine white charger, had made a stirring speech to his assembled army and been loudly cheered.

Everything, said the spies, told clearly that the great army would begin its advance at dawn.

Chapter Three

There was time in hand for the Swaynes to make their final preparations.

The Earl's army had fifteen miles to come. There were hills and marshy streams to cross and the roads were rough and narrow. With their heavy, loaded wagons and ponderous siege weapons, Swayne reckoned they would camp the night half way and arrive next evening.

The town people had already gone to their emergency quarters in the surrounding farms and fishing villages. The houses were barred and shuttered. Only the castle garrison remained.

Swayne put them to the final clearing of the woodlands around the castle. Strenuous work relieved the suspense of waiting. Scouts kept him well posted of the Earl's advance. The cavalcade, as expected, had set out at dawn.

When his men broke for their midday meal, Swayne and Roger went up to the watch tower on the summit of the keep. Far away on the northern horizon they could see a brown haze against the summer sky: the dust clouds rising from the approaching army.

By sunset the last of the trees and brushwood had been cut down, leaving a clear space around the ramparts to deny all cover for the enemy.

At nightfall the garrison camped in a meadow outside the castle walls: cooking their food over braziers and sleeping in the open air. They would have to live behind those massive walls for long enough. Swayne wanted them to have a final night in freedom.

At midnight he took Roger to the watch tower, and they saw

the distant glow of camp fires where the Earl's army was resting for the night.

There was little to be done next morning. The cows and the goats were driven across the drawbridge: a useful load of rabbits was brought in from snares around the castle. The cattle had been kept until the last moment from that precious grazing land inside.

The only house in the town that had remained occupied until that morning was Father Peter's where Gregory had been kept under guard. As the garrison began moving in they saw the small party coming across the fields. Father Peter was to be the only non-combatant in the garrison. He was old to withstand the rigours of a siege, but the one whom Swayne could least have spared. He had been a monk at Crowland Abbey until the Swaynes built their own small church. He had now been with them twenty years and his value went far beyond his priestly duties. Among other things he was schoolmaster and doctor. His skill in treating wounds would be as useful to the garrison as his other ways of keeping them in health.

He knew that a besieged garrison was more often defeated by disease within the castle than by the enemy outside. He had long foreseen these days of trial and had done what he could to meet them. He had enclosed some land behind the ramparts and planted a small vegetable garden. He now had a fine crop of cabbages and kale. He had put the town boys on to netting the nearby river to stock the moat with fish, and had planted the sides of the moat with watercress. Prayers, he told Swayne, were excellent for the soul, but when a stomach was bound up by salt meat and coarse bread a handful of watercress was worth a power of praying. He had gathered wild fruit and berries, boiled them with honey to a syrup, and sealed this in stone jars.

Above all else was the man himself. He was fat and cheerful, never got excited or lost his temper, and saw the funny side of the most unlikely things. He was a sort of Friar Tuck, and everybody liked him.

Roger was at the gatehouse when Father Peter arrived with Gregory. He hadn't seen Gregory since the skirmish on the river bank and now had a special reason for taking a closer look at him. There was a dungeon in the vaults for prisoners, but scarcely the place for a boy who wasn't even captured in an act of war. Swayne had therefore decided that Gregory should share the small room in the keep that he had set aside for his son. Roger had objected. He wanted the room to himself. But his father had pointed out that if it hadn't been for Roger they wouldn't have the Earl's son on their hands.

'So the least you can do,' he said, 'is to help look after him.'

Roger had reluctantly agreed, but when he saw Gregory arrive at the castle he took an instant and profound dislike to him.

He came swaggering across the drawbridge as if the castle belonged to him: more like a conqueror than a captive. When one of his guards touched his arm to direct him towards the keep he looked at the man in haughty disdain and brushed his sleeve as if wiping away something unclean.

'He thinks he owns the earth,' said Roger. 'I'd sooner sleep on the grass outside than share a room with him.'

Swayne saw the point. 'You can sleep in my room for the time being,' he said, and Roger was content.

There was a grinding of winches and a straining of chains as the drawbridge was heaved up, and the garrison was ready. War seemed remote on that quiet summer afternoon. A few gulls wheeled lazily overhead, the cattle grazed placidly around the keep, the sunlight glistened on the distant sea. Even the castle looked drowsy in the August heat: nothing to show what labour had been spent upon its preparation for the siege. The outer ramparts, strengthened and repaired, dropped sheer to the moat that encircled the redoubt. A narrow path along its parapet, with a breastwork for protection, provided a track for patrolling sentries.

Towering above all else was the massive stone keep: the ultimate stronghold if an enemy breached the outer defences. It stood like a rock, fifty feet high, in the centre of the enclosure, and so far as the skill of its builders could achieve, it was impregnable.

Its only entrance was by a narrow door twelve feet above ground level, reached by a flight of wooden steps which could be pulled up in emergency. The door led into the guardroom where the garrison lived and slept. Beneath this was the kitchen. Below that, deep in the foundations, were the storerooms and the well.

Above the guardroom was the main hall, the only place in the fortress with any pretensions to comfort and display. The topmost floor was divided into four small rooms for those with work that needed freedom from the activities below. One was for Swayne himself: a command post where he could work and sleep. A few steps led up to the watch tower on the summit of the keep from which he could see every part of the castle under his command, with a wide view beyond, over the surrounding country.

There was a room for Father Peter, with shelves and cupboards for his medicines and dressings. He was also in charge of stores, with a duty to keep careful check on provisions dealt out to the cooks for daily rations.

The third room was for the officers in charge of the groups into which the garrison was divided. The fourth had been intended for conferences, but when Swayne had decided to let Roger stay he had assigned this room to him, which now he was to share with Gregory.

To allow more living space inside the fortress, a projecting turret with a narrow spiral stairway served all floors from the vaults to the watch tower. The fortress had been built in an iron-hard stone quarried from the ruins of a Roman town nearby. At its base the walls were four feet thick; almost to its summit they spanned a yard. The builders had searched the forests miles around for the oak to provide its massive beams. It was proof, the men said, against everything but God and the Devil.

Swayne had reckoned that the Earl's army would be in sight by mid-day but it was apparently finding it slow going, and to ease the strain of waiting he began the siege routine.

The garrison was divided into four groups of eight men, each to stand watch for two hours. Four would patrol the ramparts, two would be on the parapet above the gatehouse and two at the watch tower on the summit of the keep. Each group was in charge of an officer who moved around among them. The cooks were free from guard duties, but on hand for the ramparts in emergency.

With the first watch posted there was no more to do but wait. Two men went through the narrow pass door at the gatehouse and set the nets and lines in the moat for fish. The man in charge of the poultry collected a few eggs; another milked the cows and Father Peter cut some cabbages from his garden to go with the evening meal. A target was set up, and the men off duty exercised themselves in bowmanship.

They were young and new to war. Their spirits were high, looking forward to a great adventure.

It was near sunset when the Earl's army at last appeared in sight. It came over a low hill crest half a mile away.

At the head of the column marched the mercenaries, led by their Captain, Raymond of Bethune. Tough, hard-bitten soldiers, well-disciplined and armed, marching with a steady, swinging rhythm. Next came the Earl himself, magnificently arrayed, riding his white battle horse, surrounded by a mounted escort.

Then came the levies from the Earl's estates, marching in groups under their own leaders. They were well equipped, but made a poor showing after the impressive company of mercenaries. There was a long cavalcade of wagons loaded with stores, munitions and equipment; ponderous siege engines; a great wooden tower drawn by a dozen straining oxen.

Finally came a mixed assortment of non-combatants: cooks and servants, carpenters and blacksmiths and men of all work for the camp. Watching from the summit of the keep Swayne reckoned that the Earl's army, all told, must number nearly a thousand men.

Compared with modern war with its screaming jets and roaring tanks the opening to the siege of Swayne Castle was a strangely quiet, sedate affair. The most powerful siege engines of the day could scarcely throw a projectile beyond 200 yards. The strongest bowman could rarely shoot an arrow beyond that distance. So when the Earl halted and surveyed the castle from less than a quarter mile he was in perfect safety.

Proceedings began with a ceremony traditional on such occasions.

The Earl sent forward a mounted herald, resplendently attired. From the far side of the moat he saluted Lord Swayne and read in a loud voice the Royal warrant, declaring Lord Swayne a rebel and ordering him to surrender the castle to the Earl as the King's appointed deputy.

Swayne answered briefly. 'Tell your master that I am no rebel. I have never declared myself against the King and shall never do so. The warrant you have read was extracted from the King by fraud and slander to serve the Earl's own ends. On that account I refuse to accept it.'

And that was that. The herald saluted and rode away.

The Earl watched these proceedings with some anxiety. It sometimes happened that a besieged commander would demand the right to a Royal hearing, to plead his case directly before the King. Worse still, so far as the Earl was concerned, would have been if Swayne had tamely surrendered. This would have been a miserable fiasco after the Earl's costly preparations, cheating him out of a longed-for opportunity to prove his military skill by the spectacular capture of the castle.

He was therefore much relieved and gratified by Swayne's defiance and set about his work with vigour. He rode around the ramparts of the castle with his officers, keeping well beyond range of any missiles that might be aimed at him. He chose positions every hundred yards or so and directed sentries to pitch tents and settle in. The castle was soon surrounded by a wide circle of guard posts, sealing it off from any attempt to send out messengers or bring in stores or reinforcements under cover of night.

The Earl's main encampment was set up by the river about half a mile away. The tents were unloaded. The cooks made fires; men began drawing water from the river.

The Earl chose a good position for his own headquarters, on a low ridge as near to the castle as he could come with safety. It was a sound strategic position with the whole field of operations in view. He was doing things in style. Some wagons drew up and heavy rolls of fabric were unloaded, spread out on the ground and strung together. A wooden framework was constructed, and workmen with the aid of ladders drew the fabric over it to make the biggest and most resplendent tent that Swayne's men had ever seen.

It was an ornamental pavilion rather than a tent. On grand occasions when the barons were called to Royal assemblies, they took their own pavilions with them, and the Earl, who liked his comfort, had brought his for the siege. It made an impressive show, standing there on the ridge with the setting sun behind it, the Earl's banner flying proudly overhead.

Swayne's men watched the furnishings carried in: a luxurious bed, carved wooden chairs with tapestried coverings, a long heavy table, silver candelabra and tableware. Thinking of their cramped quarters in the castle and the frugal food awaiting them, the garrison admitted that the Earl had got the best of it so far.

Swayne was less interested in the Earl's spectacular pavilion than in what was going on behind it. Although they had cleared the ground around the castle they couldn't alter the contours of the land. Behind the Earl's pavilion ran a narrow valley, a deep depression out of sight of the castle, even from the watch tower on the keep.

The Earl had directed a number of wagons into this valley, stacked with what from a distance looked like timber framework. Swayne heard the clatter of unloading, then a steady, ceaseless hammering. It was obviously something to do with an impending attack, and Swayne would have given a lot to know what it was.

It began to grow dark: another hot summer night with a mutter of thunder in the distance and a flicker of summer lightning. The garrison could see fires glowing in the encampment by the river. They could hear men singing. All around them, evenly spaced out, they saw the yellow blur of lanterns in the guard tents.

The Earl's pavilion stood out clearly in the darkness. The entrance facing the castle had been drawn back to let in the cool night air and Swayne's men had a clear view of what was going on inside. The Earl was entertaining his officers to dinner. The long table was lit by lanterns. Servants were going in and out with dishes of food and flagons of wine. Through the darkness came the sound of a minstrel playing.

Swayne guessed that the Earl had deliberately opened up his pavilion to display his pomp and power; to throw a gesture of contempt at the people he would shortly overwhelm.

It was clear enough that no attack was contemplated that night. Swayne told his officers to relax the alert and return to normal siege routine.

'Get the men off duty to bed in the guardroom,' he said. 'The more sleep they have tonight the better.'

At midnight he took Roger with him for the changing of the guard. As Roger carried the lantern to light the way he thought back on those exciting exploits with his boy companions, defending the empty castle against imaginary enemies whom they invariably routed with great loss. Reality was strangely different. So far not a thing had happened. The enemy hadn't shot a single arrow or flung the smallest missile at the castle. The army had settled in beside the river and the Earl had entertained his officers to a sumptuous banquet as if Swayne Castle didn't exist.

Yet there was romance in that night patrol around the ramparts. Not a sound came from that great Army out there in the darkness. He could see a few dying camp fires by the river and the faint glow from the lanterns inside the guard tents that surrounded them. Sometimes an owl hooted, and a fox was barking in the distant woods. There was a mutter of far-off thunder and the lapping of the sea as the tide came in.

Swayne had a few words with the sentries and a talk with the officer of the watch. When the round was made he said to Roger, 'I shan't be coming to my room till dawn, but it's time you turned in and got some sleep.'

Roger went to the keep and climbed the steep winding steps to the top floor where he was to sleep in his father's room. In the narrow passage he stopped and listened at the padlocked door of the small room where Gregory was imprisoned. There was no sound. If Gregory were still awake, Roger wondered what he was thinking about in his loneliness, and had half a mind to call out 'Goodnight'.

Chapter Four

When dawn gave the garrison a view beyond the ramparts they expected the enemy to have brought their siege engines forward under cover of the night.

But nothing had happened. Apart from the sentries patrolling between the guard posts there was no sign of life. The Earl's pavilion was closed and silent. The army in the encampment by the river was apparently still asleep. The sun had risen before an officer with a company of men came across the meadows to relieve the sentries who had been on duty at the guard posts through the night.

The knocking and hammering began again in the hidden valley. It went on persistently for hours. The Earl came out of his pavilion, talked to some waiting officers, and walked into the valley. The mystery in that valley troubled Swayne. It had nothing to do with the siege engines. The tower stood neglected in a field nearby. Whatever was brewing down there out of sight was something Swayne hadn't allowed for.

The Earl reappeared. He mounted his warhorse and rode off with his officers to the encampment by the river.

Presently a company of soldiers assembled there and moved forward. Swayne knew from their steady rhythmic march that they were the Earl's best fighting men: his mercenaries, his shock troops. They marched across the fields and disappeared into the valley.

It was enough for Swayne to alert the garrison. He told his officers to bring them to the ramparts and take action stations.

The hammering stopped in the hidden valley. The silence was

more ominous than the noise. For half an hour the time dragged by.

When things at last began to happen they were so casual and unhurried that they seemed to have no part in an assault upon the castle. Out of the valley came a dozen workmen wheeling what looked like the steep roof taken off a barn.

Swayne recognized it as a penthouse, well known in siege warfare. A number of them, joined end to end gave cover in an advance towards a castle. The men inside could push them forward on their wheels, secure against the arrows and missiles of the defenders.

What use could they be put to now? Thrust first against the walls of a castle they gave an assault party cover to hack a way through. But they couldn't bridge a moat, and the moat around Swayne Castle was broad and deep. The whole thing, at first sight, had no sense in it.

Then came something that put an end to Swayne's uncertainty. Out of the valley came the Earl's cherished 'secret weapon'. It was drawn by a team of workmen: a mobile bridge, based upon a wheeled platform, its forward end projecting upwards like a modern crane.

The workmen manoeuvred it to face the gatehouse. A line of penthouses were fastened behind it until the whole thing looked like an enormous sea serpent, the raised bridge in front like a head with open jaws.

The sentries on the ramparts stared at the unearthly monster in astonishment. For Swayne the Earl's grand scheme was clear. The gatehouse was the most vulnerable point in the defences of a castle. To thrust the bridge across the moat against the surrounding ramparts would merely bring it up against a massive wall, but in front of the gatehouse they only had the oak doors and portcullis to cope with. Safe beneath the penthouses they could get to work with battering rams and soon break through.

So this was the Earl's 'secret weapon' and very formidable it looked. But Swayne also had a secret weapon, and now that the Earl's intentions were clear, he hurried to the gatehouse to prepare it.

When the workmen had lashed the penthouses behind the mobile bridge the company of mercenaries appeared and entered the long covered passage. The ungainly monster began to move. Strung out inside the line of penthouses the mercenaries pushed them forward on their well-oiled wheels, those in the foremost penthouse guiding the mobile bridge towards its destination.

The silence of it was uncanny. This was war in earnest, yet without a sound from the mercenaries beneath the penthouses or from the defenders on the castle walls.

The Earl had good cause to be proud of his invention. The mercenaries had been well drilled. They guided the bridge directly opposite the gatehouse and when they released its supporting ropes it spanned the moat and dropped fair and square in front of the gatehouse doors. The penthouses were pushed forward across the bridge and a battering ram was soon in action.

When the Earl heard the first crushing blows he was transported with delight. His army was at the threshold of a brilliant victory.

The doors beneath the gatehouse were thick and strong, but no doors could stand for long against the blows of a battering ram in the hands of a dozen powerful men. There was a crashing and a splintering as the locks and bars gave way, and the mercenaries surged forward with a cheer into the tunnel beneath the gatehouse.

To the Earl, from his vantage point on the nearby ridge, the cheers came as a triumphant call of victory.

What he hadn't allowed for was the inventive genius of King Henry Plantagenet, who had designed the castle many years before. Usually the archway beneath the gatehouse led directly into the castle, but in this case the King had given it more depth than width. Beyond the doors was a stone-flagged tunnel thirty feet long, with a portcullis at the farther end.

Above this tunnel was a small room with apertures in its floor covering with iron sheeting that could be drawn aside. In this room Swayne now had braziers glowing white hot with charcoal steeped in oil. Above the braziers were cauldrons filled with boiling grease. Half a dozen of Swayne's men stood around them.

For Swayne it was a nerve-racking ordeal. To give the word too soon the weapon would be thrown away; too late would mean disaster and defeat.

When the mercenaries poured through the broken doors they saw the portcullis at the far end of the tunnel. They had not allowed for a second barrier, but saw it only as a temporary obstruction. The ram would soon break through it.

They were too intent upon their work to notice that the iron coverings in the roof above had been removed. Had they looked up they could scarcely have seen the apertures in the gloom.

Swayne, looking down, could see the attackers labouring forward with the ram to destroy the portcullis. The rest of the mercenaries were crowding in from the penthouses behind, ready to surge through into the castle when the portcullis was destroyed.

Swayne held his hand: waiting for the whole company to be packed into the tunnel.

The ram crashed against the portcullis, but the barrier held firm. It was withdrawn for the second blow and during that time Swayne saw that the last of the mercenaries had crowded into the tunnel. All they now waited for was the blow of the ram that destroyed the portcullis and gave them a triumphant entry.

But before the second blow was aimed Swayne gave the word.

The cauldrons of boiling grease were lifted with iron bars and tilted through the open hatchways onto the crowded mercenaries. There were shouts of alarm and cries of pain. The grease had scalded a few of them, and the unharmed men prepared to attack the portcullis with redoubled energy.

The second blow never came. Swayne's men followed up the boiling grease with sacks of oil-soaked tinder and flaming torches lit from the brazier fires. In an instant the tunnel beneath them was a holocaust: a raging furnace filled with black oily smoke and flames. And Swayne's men made assurance doubly sure by stoking the furnace with more sacks of oil-soaked tinder.

Their deadly work done, they drew the iron sheets across the apertures to save being suffocated.

Swayne's next move came on the spur of the moment. From the window he had seen the Earl's levies massing on the distant hill crest. It was clearly the Earl's design to let the mercenaries break in before sending his levies forward in a grand assault to share the victory.

They could never get through that furnace in the tunnel, but the mobile bridge and penthouses were still in place. If the levies could establish themselves in the penthouses they could renew the attack when the flames burnt down, and Swayne decided upon a hazardous mission.

Some steps led down to a narrow door beside the moat. From there it was only a few yards to the penthouses and bridge. The six men in the room took the iron bars from the cauldrons, some sacks of tinder and lighted torches and followed Swayne down the steps. They attacked the penthouses furiously with the iron bars, broke jagged holes and thrust the sacks of tinder in with the flaming torches. The hot summer weather was on their side. The penthouses were bone dry and burnt like matchwood. In a few moments there was a roaring blaze.

The work was well done but at a price. Some mercenaries who had escaped from the holocaust in the tunnel attacked Swayne's men with a fury stoked by pain. They were a terrifying sight with their clothes aflame: and Swayne's men fought back with their iron bars, striving to break through to the narrow door that led into the gatehouse.

Swayne reached the door with three of his men, but the others were overwhelmed and cut down by the mercenaries. To go back to their help was suicide. They were beyond help anyway. Swayne ordered his surviving men through the open door and thrust the bar across.

From the battlements above he saw the surviving mercenaries come staggering out of the tunnel, charred by the flames, their burning clothes turning them into blazing torches. Half-blinded they groped for escape towards the mobile bridge, but finding it a mass of flame, threw themselves into the moat. The water hissed from their burning clothes and sent up clouds of steam.

The Earl, with an eye for showmanship, had ordered his own men on to the hill crest to witness the wonders of his 'secret weapon'. When assured that the mercenaries had broken through, he would give a signal for the massed advance of his whole army to share in the glory of the victory.

The cheers of the mercenaries as they broke down the gates was the moment the Earl had waited for. He gave the signal, and the whole army surged forward, cheering and waving their swords as they raced down the hillside.

He was so intrigued by the glorious charge that he did not at first see the black smoke billowing up around the gatehouse. Then to his horror he saw the penthouses and mobile bridge ablaze.

He stood there, dazed and helpless. His unwieldy army was now completely beyond control, racing towards the gatehouse, yelling with excitement. Discipline had gone with the wind. The leaders were lost in the crowd and the fastest runners got there first. When they reached the moat they stopped and stared in bewilderment at the mass of flame that had been the bridge.

For Swayne's men, on the ramparts, it was a gift beyond belief. They had been forbidden to waste arrows on the penthouses, but here was a heavensent target. They were good bowmen and now proved it with a vengeance.

As the levies came crowding down to the far side of the moat they stood there like a herd of stampeded cattle brought up against a wall, and Swayne's men poured a deadly hail of arrows into them. The leaders attempted to get them away, but the men at the back were still pressing forward, and there was chaos.

It wasn't to be all honey for those jubilant young men on the ramparts.

Some of the mercenaries had not gone forward to attack the gatehouse. They had taken stations on the flanks to deal with any defenders who might expose themselves on the castle walls. In their ardour to shoot down the helpless levies Swayne's men were standing on the battlements to give them better aim, and were an easy target for expert mercenary bowmen.

The first to fall were scarcely noticed by their companions. So intent were they upon the slaughter of the helpless levies that they were not aware of the fierce retaliation from the flanks. Several had fallen before the officers dragged the others down to the protection of the breastworks.

The battle was soon over. Panic had seized the disordered levies. They were racing back faster, if anything, than they had come. The ground was strewn with fallen men: the moat still steamed from the quenched flames of the shattered bridge and a pall of black smoke hung above the gatehouse. The sea murmured in the distance and a few gulls flapped overhead in blissful unconcern.

It had been a splendid victory for the garrison, but with no cause for celebration when they began to count the cost.

A corner of the guardroom was curtained off for the badly wounded men and Father Peter, with the light of lanterns, began the agonizing work of removing barbed arrowheads deeply embedded in the flesh. He was skilled in treating the wounds of people injured in their normal work, but these arrow wounds were as torturing for him as for the men he tried to help.

Outside, in a corner of the meadow, they buried their dead.

A final task remained, and the sooner it was done the better. The tunnel beneath the gatehouse had to be cleared, and Swayne chose two of his older, hardened men to help him: the butcher and the blacksmith.

The smoke had cleared, but the stones were black with soot and the tunnel stiflingly hot. The bodies were scarcely recognizable as human. Some lay pinned beneath the smouldering ram that sent up a splutter of sparks when rolled aside. There was no likelihood of a night attack after that resounding beating. It was safe enough to lower the drawbridge and carry the bodies across on hurdles. They laid them in a row beyond the castle walls. With a grappling iron they dragged a dozen bodies from the moat, put them beside the others, and the revolting task was done.

Swayne sent word for his officers to come to his room at the summit of the keep, and it wasn't until he was climbing the steep winding stairs that he had time to think of Roger.

He had known from the start that Roger would be a problem when the ramparts were attacked. If he were left free he would be up there with the men, trying to do heroic deeds to prove his courage. Swayne wanted him as future leader of his people, not to bury him. He had hit upon a plan to keep the boy out of danger without making him think he was being tucked away for safety.

'I'm putting you in charge of the watch tower,' he had said. 'I think the main attack will be against the gatehouse. But there may be a surprise assault against another part of the ramparts. If you see that developing, you must sound the alarm to give the garrison a warning.'

It gave the boy a useful job and Roger went off proudly to his lonely vigil on the summit of the keep.

All day he had stood there watching for a sign of the enemy gathering for an attack from the fringes of the woodlands. He had heard the clamour around the gatehouse and seen the black smoke rising, but knew that his father and the garrison were taking care of this. His duty was to stand guard over the unprotected stretches of the ramparts. Towards evening his eyes began to ache from straining through the twilight.

All through that critical day Swayne had no time to think of Roger except that he was mercifully beyond sight of the horrible carnage. It was only now that he realized that the boy had been up there for hours without relief. He went up the turret steps, and there was the exhausted Roger, fast asleep on the platform beside the battlement.

The boy was full of contrition when his father woke him up. He began to apologize for failing in his duty but his father assured him that he had done a fine job. The worst was over, victory had been won.

'And now,' said his father, 'you deserve a good night's rest.'

Roger was still sleeping on a mattress in a corner of his father's room. 'My officers are coming here for a talk,' said Swayne, 'but I think you're too tired for it to disturb you.'

Roger lay down and pulled a blanket around him. When the four officers came in they saw the boy huddled up, apparently fast asleep, but what his father said to them made sleep impossible, and Roger lay there listening to every word of it.

'When we prepared for this siege,' Swayne told them, 'we decided that forty men was the barest minimum to garrison this castle. We cut it to bedrock to conserve our food supplies.

'Six have been killed today and four so badly wounded that they'll never fight again. To hold this castle with thirty men would mean such a heavy burden of extra duties that it would wear them out, even if we had no further attacks to meet.

'The Earl's losses are nothing compared with ours. He can easily hire new mercenaries and reinforce the levies from his estates. He'll throw everything against us to revenge this defeat and we haven't a chance with a tired garrison fighting under strength.

'Also, these badly wounded men will never survive if they stay here, lying in the guardroom, and it's demoralizing for the others to have tortured, groaning men beside them when they try to sleep.'

Swayne told them of his plan.

In the nearest fishing village three miles down the coast were good men who would gladly join the garrison. A messenger must get through to tell them what had happened. On the following night a dozen must come as reinforcements along the coast path, four fishing boats alongside them. The wounded men would be ready on stretchers, and in the brief summer hours of darkness a double operation must be carried out: the wounded taken to the waiting fishing boats and the reinforcements brought in.

It was a plan that depended upon a fragile thread of chance and luck, but with careful timing Swayne believed it possible. He explained the intricate details to his officers. First they must choose the messenger, who would have to go next night. He had to be alert: resourceful: intelligent enough to carry the instructions in his head. They finally decided upon a young man named Rolf. 'He's quick witted,' one said. 'He can run like a hare. Just the fellow we need.'

'Very well,' said Swayne. 'Send Rolf to me in the morning.'

Lying there in his dark corner, apparently asleep, Roger could scarcely contain his indignation when no one even mentioned him as a possible messenger. He was the one for the job, and he nearly jumped up and said so. But to interrupt the conference would probably have ruled him out, so he waited until the others had gone, and his father was alone.

He sat up on his mattress and said, 'Why not me?'

His father was surprised and angry.

'I thought you were asleep,' he said. 'When I gave you permission to sleep in my room it wasn't for you to listen to meetings with my officers.'

'How could I help listening?' retorted Roger.

'What we were discussing was no concern of yours.'

'When you made me one of the garrison,' said Roger, 'you said I must do whatever jobs I was fit for. Why shouldn't I take the message to the fishing village?'

'Because we have chosen Rolf,' said Swayne.

'Why Rolf – when I can do it?'

'Rolf is older than you.'

Roger let himself go. 'You don't have to be old to carry a message!' he shot back. 'Rolf doesn't know the way to the fishing village as well as I do. I've explored along the coast by night a dozen times. I know every yard of it. If Rolf got lost, then what do you do? I can run as fast as Rolf, and swim much better. If the Earl's men got a sight of me I know places to hide, and if it came to it I could wade out and swim the rest of the way.'

Swayne was up against it. If only he had sent the confounded boy to that monastery and got rid of him! If the Earl were to capture him he wouldn't treat him as Swayne was treating Gregory. But there was good sense and reason in what Roger said. He knew that coast like the palm of his hand. The message was not a simple one. It contained vital details easier to explain to his son than to Rolf who might in the excitement get it garbled.

So Swayne agreed that his son should be the messenger.

'Now go to sleep,' he said. 'You won't get any tomorrow night.'

Early next morning Roger was out on the ramparts watching the movements of the sentries at the guard tents. The tents were about a hundred yards apart and the sentries followed a fixed routine. They would walk slowly from one tent to the next, pass the time of day with the neighbouring sentry, and then walk back again.

If they followed the same routine at night, then Roger saw no difficulty. He would make for a position between two of the guard tents, lie in wait for the sentry to pass, and slip through before he returned. But at night they might work with double patrols, or with sentries at fixed stations between the guard tents. That he would have to risk, trusting to the darkness and his speed in running. From the ramparts that morning he chose for his break-through a position where the surrounding woodlands encroached nearest to the guard tents. Once through the lines he could race for the woods that stretched almost to the sea coast.

All afternoon, in his father's room, he memorized every detail of the plan. Swayne told him the names of the men he wanted as reinforcements; how they must be equipped, how the fishing boats were to be adapted to take the stretchers of the wounded men. Timing was the keystone, but so many unseen hazards lay ahead that little could be settled in advance. They needed signals that wouldn't rouse suspicion. The owls were active in the woods at that time of the year, and Roger, who knew his woodcraft, said that when they called their mates they always gave a short hoot followed by a long one. Roger's call would be the other way round: long, then short. Nobody in the Earl's army was likely to spot the difference. The first signal would come from the woods when he was safely through the enemy lines; the second on the following night, when the critical operation was to begin.

Towards evening Roger got ready for his journey. He dressed in clothes that would blend with the darkness: blue trunks that fitted closely from foot to waist, and a dark brown shirt. He wanted to black his face and hands with charcoal, but Swayne said, 'No. If you sweat, the charcoal will run down into your eyes. Your sunburn is sufficient.'

He would carry no arms. He suggested a dagger, but Swayne again said, 'No. A dagger needs a sheath that needs a belt. Anything that gets in the way or makes a sound is out. You've got to be as quiet as a mouse, as slippery as an eel and as fast as a hare.'

So Roger had nothing but his trunks and shirt and shoes, and the message locked safely in his memory.

It was a dark moonless night, very still and quiet. They went through the pass door at the gatehouse and ferried Roger across the moat. A whispered 'Good luck' and he was out in no-man's-land, between the castle and the enemy guard tents. A short way from the castle he saw a black stick planted in the ground. He stopped, and approached it warily, suspecting some sort of trap attached to an alarm. On closer inspection he saw that it was an arrow with its head buried in the ground: shot by the garrison the previous day.

He was guided by the faint glow of the lanterns in the guard tents and made for a point midway between the two tents nearest to the woodlands. As he got closer he went down on his knees and crawled. Presently he heard the unexpected sound of music. It came from one of the tents close to the path that the sentry used on his patrol. He lay flat on his stomach, peering ahead and listening. The music stopped, but there was a droning talk, sometimes a short laugh. All manner of possibilities ran through Roger's mind. Had they altered their methods at night? Laid traps across the land between the guard tents to catch an intruder like a rabbit? Or perhaps they had seen him coming, and were simply waiting for him to crawl out of the darkness? If they hadn't seen him, then surely they would hear him now, for his heart was beating like a drum.

At last it happened. Out of the darkness loomed a sentry. He paused much closer to Roger than he had allowed for: about five paces away. Roger buried himself in the grass and held his breath. The sentry was evidently quite unperturbed. He was humming the tune that the man had played on the guitar, and he stopped and scratched his back with his sword.

Roger barely waited for him to disappear into the darkness. He began to crawl forward as stealthily as a cat. He was soon on the beaten path that the sentries had worn down. A few more yards and he was through. He leapt to his feet and went streaking towards the woods expecting a shout of warning and a stampede of the

Earl's men after him. But there was no sound from the sentry lines. He plunged into the woods and embraced the first tree in thankfulness. When he had got his breath back he filled his lungs and let go the two triumphant hoots that the castle was waiting for. No owl could have done better.

He was soon on the woodland path that led down to the sea. He came out on the coast where a desolate stretch of marshland reached back from the sea, but a firm path lay between the shingle and the marshes. He was out in the open now; no cover beyond a few stunted, stormbent trees. If the enemy had established a watch post on that narrow path he would be in a bad way, for the marshes were perilous with quicksand, and the sea a doubtful alternative for escape. But as his eyes became accustomed to the darkness he could see the path was clear ahead, and the farther he went the less he feared an enemy guard post.

It was fine to smell the sea again and hear it lapping on the shingle. He ran with an easy stride along the coast path, enjoying the freedom of the open night.

Chapter Five

What was happening meanwhile in the camp of the besieging army?

With his cherished 'secret weapon' burnt to ashes and nothing ready to take its place the Earl was up against a problem with his levies. He had assured them that the campaign would be a short, triumphant one: that the men would be home in good time for the harvest.

By feudal law he could only call upon them for forty days' military service in the year. They would soon have every right to pack and go, and after the carnage around the gatehouse they would be all the happier to wash their hands of it.

But his worst fears concerned his mercenary Captain, Raymond of Bethune. He resented not having full command, and had been half-hearted about the Earl's 'secret weapon'. Now that the thing had been a disastrous failure, and forty of his men had been lost in the holocaust, what would Raymond do now?

If he resigned in disgust, the Earl's position would be appalling. The whole campaign depended upon the mercenaries. He couldn't hope to take Swayne Castle with an army of inexperienced amateurs, all wanting to get home.

Everything depended upon Raymond, and he sent for him to come to the pavilion.

He walked in without the usual salutation, and when the Earl offered him a cup of wine he looked at him in contempt and turned away.

The Earl nearly burst with indignation. He had never been insulted like this in his life, but Raymond held the power.

'I have lost,' he said, 'forty of my best men. They had fought under my command through many victorious campaigns and can never be replaced. They were thrown away on a futile experiment that I told you from the beginning wouldn't work.

'Apart from this loss,' he said, 'there is the damage to my own prestige. I carried out this foolish experiment because I was in your employ, but I shall be held to blame for its failure. When it becomes known that I have lost these men in a crushing defeat, how will my reputation stand on the Continent?'

The Earl was fighting for his own reputation and far more. If Raymond deserted him the siege would collapse like a stack of cards.

'It is a temporary setback,' he said, 'not a crushing defeat. I am determined to take this castle, and with your help I am certain of it. I have the money to pay a thousand mercenaries if need be, and place them under your command. But if you were to leave me . . .'

Raymond broke in with a flash of anger, but he knew that he had got the Earl where he wanted him.

'When I accept a commission I undertake to bring victory with it. I have never yet broken my promise, and shall not do so now. I shall remain in your employment until this castle is taken. No power on earth will stop me from avenging this defeat.'

The Earl could scarcely contain his relief, but Raymond's terms were yet to come. The Earl had money, and Raymond intended to make good use of it.

'Firstly,' he said, 'there will be compensation for the men I have lost. You will pay me an indemnity of two months' wages for every man who died.'

The demand hit the Earl where it hurt. He was fond of his money and hated spending it. He had gone into this adventure convinced that the capture of the Swayne property would more than repay the cost, but now a mountain of expenses was looming up ahead. He had a great fortune stored away in the vaults of his castle, and money was the symbol of his power.

Raymond laid down the rest of his hard terms.

'I must replace my losses,' he told the Earl. 'I cannot fight without a full company of three hundred men. I shall send to Flanders to a friend of mine who has good mercenaries available.'

Truth to tell, the disaster at the gatehouse wasn't such a personal calamity as Raymond had made out. Had it been a success his employment would have been over in a week, with no more work for his men until next summer. But the siege, as he now envisaged it, would keep his men profitably employed at the Earl's expense.

'If I do this for you,' he said, 'I must be in full control of future operations. I cannot fight with one hand tied behind my back. In return I promise that I shall not leave until I have handed over to you the captured castle.'

The Earl was so relieved that he would have agreed to almost anything, but he could not agree to handing over the whole command to Raymond, lock, stock and barrel. He pointed out that his own retainers were bound to him by feudal law. He must remain their commander, if only in name.

Raymond agreed. He had a poor impression of the levies anyway. When it came to fighting he didn't want to have them getting in his way.

It was therefore arranged that the Earl should remain officially the Commander of the whole army including the mercenaries. He would look after administration and supplies but in all military matters Raymond was to have a free hand.

So Raymond went back to his tent, well pleased with his morning's work, and the Earl took in hand the awkward problem of his retainers.

He knew it would be a tricky business, so he laid on a special lunch, with plenty of good wine to sweeten his retainers up. He led off with the good news that Raymond would stand firm until the Swaynes were defeated. This pleased the retainers, who had a lurking fear that the mercenaries might pack up and leave the Earl's own men to bear the brunt.

Then came the problem of the harvest. Fine crops were standing in the fields, ready for the reapers. A spell of bad weather would ruin them. It was vital to get them in.

The Earl had in fact more levies than he strictly needed. Four hundred would be ample with the mercenaries standing in, so he agreed to release three hundred for the harvest.

The question of money then arose. The tenants had to pay the wages of their men during the forty days of feudal service, but after that, what happened? After some hard bargaining the Earl agreed to pay a penny a day for every man engaged upon the siege, he bearing the cost of their upkeep.

And so it was settled, The tenants went away to arrange what men should be released for the harvest, and the Earl was left to face the shocking cost of it.

He sent for his Treasurer, a tall, gaunt man as tight-fisted as his master.

'I must have,' said the Earl, 'an exact account upon how we stand and what we have already spent and how the money we are now committed to will measure up against our reserves.'

The Treasurer had all the figures, down to the last penny. He had brought with him an armful of scrolls that he spread out on the table.

The currency in those days was a thin little silver coin called a penny but worth far more than a penny of today. Tenants paid the Earl according to the value of the land they held, and after an allowance for expenses the rest was stored in the castle vaults in leather bags called 'satchels'. Each satchel contained a thousand pennies: carefully sealed and recorded in the Treasurer's accounts.

'Before you embarked upon this campaign,' said the Treasurer, 'you had 467 satchels in the vaults.'

It was a princely hoard. King John no doubt would have been happy if the Royal treasury had had half as much.

'The initial expenses,' announced the Treasurer, 'were heavy. You employed carpenters to build the siege engines and women to cut and sew the uniforms for the levies. There were tents for the encampment; lanterns; cooking utensils; weapons and materials, and the cost of feeding your army during its training.'

He added up the figures and said, 'On the day you left the castle to begin the siege you had spent 69,000 pennies.'

The Earl was aghast. 'It couldn't have been all that! There must be some mistake!'

'It's all down here,' said the Treasurer. 'The figures carefully checked by my clerks.'

'We come now to the running costs of the siege,' he continued. 'You agreed to pay Raymond sixpence a day for his men. I told you at the time that I considered it excessive.'

'It's the price one pays to hire the best,' replied the Earl.

'That may be so,' said the Treasurer. 'But three hundred mercenaries at sixpence a day amounts to 12,600 pennies a week. Four hundred levies at a penny a day adds up to 2,800. Provisioning the army cannot be done for less than 12,000 a week. Allowing for the expenses of your officers, you cannot possibly sustain this siege at less than 30,000 pennies a week.'

This was awful. The Earl felt sick and panic stricken. He saw his magnificent fortune draining away at more than 4,000 pence a day!

'It means,' said the Treasurer, 'that if this siege is prolonged until Christmas, we shall be drawing the last satchels of money from your castle vaults.'

It hit the Earl like a hammer blow. To be destitute, penniless, when once he had been among the richest noblemen in England!

'But it won't last that long!' he cried. 'Nowhere near that long! My mercenary Captain has promised a quick victory.'

'From what I know of your mercenary Captain,' was the Treasurer's dry response, 'this siege will go on for as long as he can make good money out of it.'

When Roger reached the fishing village, some men were hauling in a boat. One was Alan Brackland whom Swayne wanted as leader of the reinforcements.

Alan was shocked to see the dishevelled, exhausted boy. His first thought was that disaster had overtaken the castle and that Roger was a solitary survivor. He was enormously relieved when Roger reassured him.

'We saw great clouds of black smoke rising in the distance,' Alan said. 'Some thought the Whole castle was aflame.' He took Roger to his hut, gave him a steaming bowl of oyster stew, and listened to the instructions that Swayne had sent.

There was nothing to be done that night. The whole of next day lay ahead to prepare the boats and muster the reinforcements. Roger was caked with dirt from his crawl through the sentry lines, drenched with perspiration from his long run through the sultry night. He took off his clothes to dry before the fire and went down to the sea for a swim.

The tide was coming in: small waves were slapping against the shingle, pushing a rim of seaweed ahead of them. When they had gone into the castle and closed the gates Roger had not expected to be close to the sea again for many a long day. It was like meeting an old friend again. He would have crawled through those guard posts any time for that long cool swim on a summer night. It relaxed and refreshed him, cleared his mind for the hazardous adventure that lay ahead.

When Swayne heard those triumphant owl calls from the woods he heaved a thankful sigh that Roger was safely through the cordon, but it was only the first move in the long series that would become increasingly perilous as the hours went by.

There was still no certainty that Roger would get safely to the fishing village; no certainty that the Earl would not launch a new attack next day, totally destroying their plan.

He had little sleep that night.

In the morning they prepared to evacuate the wounded men. It would be a painful journey over rough ground on a dark night. They made four stretchers of plaited reeds, bedded with soft grass to ease the jolting. They built a broad raft to ferry the stretchers across the moat.

The only consolation was the inactivity of the enemy. There was no movement in the Earl's encampment by the river; no sign of a new attack.

When the stretchers and raft were ready there was nothing to do but wait, and the waiting was the more intolerable with no certainty that Roger had got safely through.

They were waiting now in the fishing village. The boats were ready: the reinforcements briefed with their instructions. They couldn't stir until it was fully dark. Secrecy and silence were their only allies, night their only friend. The rowlocks of the oars were muffled; the reinforcements carried no arms or equipment that might hinder them. Each carried a thick oak bludgeon, more useful at close quarters than a sword. What a time it took for the sun to set on those long summer evenings!

As twilight began to shroud the castle the wounded men were carried from the guardroom and lain upon their stretchers. Father Peter had dressed their wounds and done what he could to make them comfortable. One, with a deep wound in his back, was lain upon his chest: another, with a shattered arm, upon his side. Wine was the only palliative in those days, and Father Peter gave them a full measure.

They were tied upon their stretchers, carried to the gatehouse and put down by the moat beside the raft.

Once again there was no more to do but wait.

Alan, leader of the relief force, stood waiting with his men for the last glow of sunset to die away.

When dark enough, he gave the word. The fishing boats were pushed out on to a calm sea and headed northwards close in to the shore. The men chosen to reinforce the garrison walked beside them along the path between the shingle and the marshland.

For a mile or more they followed the narrow causeway between the sea and marshland, desolate and silent. As they drew near their destination the marsh gave way to scrub and stunted trees then to thick woods that encroached to within a stone's throw of the shore.

They stopped here, and signalled the fishing boats to pull in. The boatmen dropped anchor some yards from the beach. It wouldn't be easy lifting the stretchers into the boats.

Roger led the reinforcements into the woods and along the track that he had come by. When they reached the fringe that faced the castle they could see the faint blur of the lanterns inside the guard tents and Roger pointed out the two marked down for capture.

When all was ready he cupped his hands and gave the two owl calls that the castle had been waiting for. The men went forward in two separate groups, making for the tents assigned to them.

This part of the plan worked perfectly. In each tent they found two men asleep. Taken completely by surprise they were gagged and bound before they were half awake.

Next came the sentries patrolling between the two guard posts. It was clear, from the ones already captured, that these men on duty around the castle were levies from the Earl's own army. Had they been trained mercenaries it would have been a different story, but amateur soldiers were easy prey. They came wandering along the sentry track, bored and half asleep. Swayne's men, lying hidden in the grass, soon had them gagged and bound: too surprised and terrified to struggle.

The gap now lay wide open, and Roger raced off to the castle gatehouse.

The call from the woods had been the signal to ferry the stretchers across the moat. They were ready there, with the bearers beside them, as Roger loomed out of the darkness. 'It's clear,' he whispered. 'I'll show you the way!'

For Roger it was an agony of suspense. Until now he had moved freely, caring only for himself or as guide to the reinforcements. But it seemed that the stretcher bearers were moving at snail's pace across the dark rough land, through the tangle of neglected uncut grass. Every minute was precious. It was barely two hundred yards from the castle to the captured guard tents, but the journey seemed interminable. Sometimes he heard a wounded man groan as a stretcher lurched and jolted, and he dreaded that one might cry out loudly in his pain.

At last he saw some men approaching through the darkness: some of the reinforcements who had come to help the stretcher bearers through. No word was spoken as they lent their help. In a minute the stretchers were safely through, on their way to the cover of the woods.

The worst half hour now lay ahead. It would take at least that time to carry the stretchers to the coast, load them on the fishing boats, and for the bearers to return. During that time the reinforcements had to keep the gap open. With the nearest sentries bound and gagged, the danger lay in the movement of the patrol from the tents beyond. Sooner or later they would come along to make contact with the sentries at the captured guard posts. If Swayne's men could dispose of these they were reasonably sure of getting the time they needed. They divided into two groups and lay in wait with gags and ropes to silence the sentries from the outer guard tents when they came along.

But now their luck deserted them. The officer in charge of the night watch probably made two rounds each night. There was a good chance of the whole operation being completed between his visits. Unfortunately it didn't work that way.

Swayne's men heard him before they saw him. He had apparently discovered some slackness among the sentries in a nearby guard post, and was upbraiding them in a loud voice. Swayne's men gripped their cudgels. There was little chance this time of springing a surprise.

Presently the officer loomed out of the darkness: a big man in chained tunic and helmet, two burly guards beside him. When he saw Swayne's men ahead he apparently took them to be sentries who had drifted together for a chat to pass the time.

He called out angrily, 'What are you doing! Get back to your posts immediately!'

One of Swayne's men took a chance and shouted, 'You are our prisoners! Lay down your arms!'

The bluff didn't work. The officer gave a sharp order to his attendants and all three disappeared into the darkness.

Immediately a loud blast from a horn shattered the silence. The alarm was taken up by another horn nearby, and again, in the distance, from the enemy's main encampment.

For Swayne, on the castle ramparts, the alarm meant the end of the plans he had devised for the whole adventure, but he had scarcely hoped for them to be carried through without mishap. His orders to Alan were to act upon his own initiative in emergency.

So Alan, out there in the darkness, with the blasts of the horns still ringing in his ears, had to make a hard decision. He could stand his ground and attempt to keep the gap open for the stretcher bearers when they returned. His chance of doing that was remote against the forces of the enemy that would answer the alarm. His men would be overwhelmed, the unarmed stretcher bearers would be rounded up, and the castle left with a mere handful of men.

He could order his men to make a headlong dash for the castle. There was a good chance of getting through before the enemy reinforcements arrived, but the stretcher bearers, with Roger their guide, would be left to their fate.

He chose a course that offered all or nothing. He ordered his men back to the woods from where they had advanced, to wait there for the stretcher bearers to return.

The journey with the stretchers down the woodland track had been slow and difficult. The path turned and twisted exhausting for the bearers in pitch darkness beneath the trees. A short journey across the open scrubland and they were there.

The boatmen had come in as close as they dared. The stretcher bearers waded in, struggling in the mud that clung to their feet. But all four stretchers were safely lifted across to the boatmen, and the boats pushed out to sea.

Their hazardous mission safely over. Roger and the bearers turned to make an easy journey back. They had crossed the scrubland and entered the woods when they heard the blasts of the enemy horns. The sound of those strident horns in the midst of a night of unbroken silence had something unearthly about it.

No sound followed: no shouts, or sound of fighting. Everything was as quiet as ever. It could only mean that their friends had been surprised and overwhelmed without a fight. To go back the way they had come would take them straight into the arms of the enemy, and Roger was for making a circuit under cover of the woods to the opposite side of the castle.

'Find a way where it's quiet,' he said. 'Make a dash through the sentry lines and swim the moat.'

Before they could start a man came running down the path towards them: one of the relief force sent to warn them of what had happened. It was good to know there hadn't been complete disaster. It put new heart into them, and they were soon back with the others.

By now a great commotion had broken out among the enemy. Orders were being shouted, lanterns were swinging in the darkness, reserves were being mustered.

Swayne's men, in the concealment of the woods, had one considerable advantage. They knew exactly what had happened while the enemy were completely in the dark. They only knew that two of the guard tents had been attacked and overwhelmed. Was it the prelude to an assault by an army to raise the siege – or an attempt by the garrison to break out? The obvious answer was to strengthen the cordon around the castle.

Roger put to Alan his idea of making through the encircling woods to the far side of the castle where a breakthrough would be least expected.

That might be possible, but Alan had another problem. It was a pitch dark night with a sea mist spreading across the fields. Even beyond the enemy cordon the castle would be engulfed in darkness. The men from the fishing village, unfamiliar with the ground, would soon be lost. Even if they got through the cordons they would have nothing to guide them. Floundering through the darkness they would probably miss the castle altogether and finish up in the enemy lines beyond.

He decided upon a mass assault, depending upon darkness and surprise, to force a way through on a narrow front.

He had a formidable force at hand: sixteen stretcher bearers: a dozen men from the fishing village: twenty-nine including Roger. In close formation they would make a powerful battering ram. He told the stretcher bearers to arm themselves with clubs from fallen branches: anything to hit out with.

He took Roger aside and said, 'You know the way to the castle blindfold. If we don't get through in the first charge, and it looks like a battle, you've got to wriggle a way through as best you can and tell the castle to light beacons.'

They went forward six abreast, shoulders almost touching. There was no picking or choosing the point for attack. A hundred yards ahead they could see the lanterns moving to and fro and hear officers shouting orders.

The first enemy to emerge from the darkness was an officer deploying some men in line, apparently part of a close cordon. Swayne's men charged in without a sound, hitting out right and left with their bludgeons. The impact was shattering. Caught off balance, completely by surprise, the cordon broke and men scattered in all directions, crying out in alarm or from the blows received.

For a few triumphant moments it seemed that they were through, with a clear run for the castle. But their luck was out. Ahead loomed a second cordon, this time a stronger one, not taken by surprise. And the shouts of alarm were bringing in a crowd of reinforcements.

Roger was at Alan's side. 'Get through,' said Alan, 'as best you can, and tell them to give us lights.'

Roger doubled back the way they had come, jumping over prostrate men stunned by the bludgeons of the first attack. He was soon clear of the fight. Racing round outside the circuit of guard tents he hoped to find a gap between the patrolling sentries, but now the whole system of patrol had been discarded, and an officer was shouting at the sentries to reinforce the fighting men. They were streaming along: all chattering and asking one another what had happened. To charge in and attempt to cross their path was too great a risk, so Roger decided to go with them. They were all too excited by the battle ahead to notice the stealthy intruder who filtered in among them.

Edging his way through the disordered crowd he was soon on the side nearest to the castle, and nobody noticed the solitary figure that parted company with them and disappeared into the darkness.

This downland, now suddenly a battlefield, had been Roger's playing ground since childhood. He could scarcely see ten yards ahead through the misty night but he knew by instinct where the castle was. He reached the moat some distance from the gatehouse but saw men on the ramparts and shouted out, 'It's Roger! They want lights to guide them! Get fires burning! Big fires! Make them blaze!'

Out there in the turmoil around the guard tents Alan and his men were surrounded and outnumbered. With no advance and no retreat Alan formed his men into a solid square, facing the enemy from all sides.

One resourceful officer could have sealed their fate with the easiest manoeuvre. He had only to withdraw his men, surround his opponents with a massive cordon and wait for daybreak to shoot them down or force surrender.

But confused night fighting wasn't likely to throw up a masterly commander. The Earl couldn't appoint a field commander over all his levies because every retainer insisted upon being in command of his own men. The result was that none of the officers knew what the others were doing and most of them had lost their own contingent in the crowd.

It didn't make it any easier for the cornered men. The crowd around them was so dense that the ones in front were shouting at those behind not to push. They had good reason to keep their distance, for in the darkness and confusion a heavy bludgeon scored more points than a sword. If an attacker was bold enough to come within distance he got a welt over the head before he could use his weapon.

Things might have gone on like this indefinitely if a small company of mounted men had not charged in to add chaos to confusion. They were the elite of the Earl's own army: retainers important enough to wear chain armour and to carry heavy swords.

They had assembled on the outskirts of the battle and now decided to complete the victory with an overwhelming charge. They came galloping out of the mist: about a dozen of them, brandishing their swords and shouting at the levies to get out of the way.

But a close-packed crowd couldn't disentangle itself at a word of command. The horsemen were blocked and submerged in a mass of jostling men. The untrained horses took fright. Some of the riders were thrown; others, in a fury to get through, slashed out in all directions with their broadswords.

It was a panic-stricken, riderless horse that broke up Alan's close-knit square. It came stampeding in among them and they had to scatter to save being trampled down. The battle now became a free-for-all. Alan's men held together in twos and threes, laying about them with their clubs, but nobody, in the mist and darkness, was now sure which were friends and which were enemies.

Then came what Alan had been praying for. A small yellow glow appeared in the distance: no bigger in the mist than the light of a lantern. Two more appeared beside it, then suddenly, as oil was poured on them they blazed up into clear beacons of flame.

They were still, for Alan's men, so near and yet so far. There was no way out of the surging crowd. They could only glimpse the lights across the heads of the attackers and fought doggedly on. The contestants were now so mixed up that some of the levies were fighting one another.

An officer hit upon a plan to single out the enemy. He got the levies to shout 'Earl's men!' as they advanced into the fray and soon the shout was taken up all round.

It didn't work the way intended. Alan's hard-pressed fighters soon got the hang of it and began shouting 'Earl's men! Earl's men!' at everybody in their way. The words were like a magic charm. The levies stood aside, and Alan's men, in twos and threes, got through the crowd and raced towards the welcoming lights on the castle ramparts. Roger was there to direct them to the raft waiting to ferry them across the moat.

There was little risk of an enemy pursuit. In the distance they could still hear the hectic shouts of 'Earl's men!' as the levies jostled about in the darkness, still looking for their opponents. The only nearby sign of what had happened were some riderless horses that had escaped from the chaos, and attracted by the beacons were placidly nibbling grass beside the moat.

The garrison had reason for festivity that night.

The victory over the mercenaries at the gatehouse had been clouded by their own grievous losses, but this was a clear-cut triumph. Their wounded were safely on their way to the fishing village and the garrison was now back to strength.

Confused nightfighting was more alarming than dangerous. Some of the men had flesh wounds and bruises, but nothing that Father Peter couldn't cope with.

Swayne had taken the brunt of the anxiety. When the sixteen

stretcher bearers had left the castle the garrison had been reduced to fourteen men. If the venture had failed, if the stretcher bearers and reinforcements had been captured, the castle would have been doomed. He called the chief cook to him and said, 'Forget rationing tonight. Prepare a supper fit for kings!'

When the fortress had been streamlined for the siege, Swayne had known that the bleak surroundings and monotonous routines would wear the men down if he didn't devise something to break the strain. For this he had given all he could to furnishing the main hall. Curtains and tapestries had been brought in from the town. The walls were decked out with emblazoned shields, stags' antlers; ancient weapons and historic banners. There were brackets in the walls for lanterns and silver ornaments for the high table. In miniature it had the feudal splendour of a proud baronial hall.

It was here that Swayne intended the garrison to dine at night. The hectic first days of the siege had ruled out this evening event, but a supper to celebrate what had happened that night was a fine opportunity to establish it.

The hall looked splendid with the lamps all glowing, revealing the rich colours of the emblems around the walls, and the cooks had prepared a dinner fit for conquerors. Into the stewing pot had gone the last of the rabbits brought in on the day the siege began: onions and carrots from Father Peter's garden, and a pudding boiled with honey and spiced with cinnamon. There was cheese and oatcakes: hard-boiled eggs, and copious wine.

The garrison was on top of the world. They drank toasts of thanks to the Earl for bungling his attempt to capture them, and were delighted to hear that the beacons that guided them home had been stoked with the shattered remains of the Earl's mobile bridge.

Roger, no doubt, received his share of praise, but he knew little about it. Long before the celebrations ended he was fast asleep.

Chapter Six

The Earl never found out what really happened on that turbulent night.

His officers gave it as their opinion that the garrison had attempted a surprise attack upon the Earl's pavilion to capture him, but that the vigilance of the guards had frustrated the attempt and seen the enemy racing back to the castle.

The Earl liked this idea. He announced that the enemy had been crushingly defeated in an attempt upon his life. He sent thanks to his army for their resolute action in defending him, and instructed his officers to double the guard around his pavilion.

Roger had now slept three nights in his father's room. So much had happened that he had been able to put off the distasteful business of meeting Gregory and trying, as his father put it to 'make friends' with him.

The more he heard about Gregory from the guards who took him his food the less he wanted to have anything to do with him. But his father was now adamant.

'You know what chivalry means in war,' he said. 'If you take a prisoner who has fought bravely you treat him with respect and courtesy. Gregory put up a stout fight before he was captured. He's not responsible for his father's attack on us, and I want you to treat him as you would like to be treated if you were in his place.'

'I'll do what I can,' said the sullen Roger, 'but if he behaves to me like he's behaved to his guards, then you mustn't blame me if he gets a black eye.'

He went down the dark passage to his room. The door was padlocked. It was Roger's sleeping room, but Gregory's prison. He unlocked the door and went in.

It was a very small room: no larger than a prison cell. Recessed in the thick wall was one narrow aperture, wide enough only for a bowman's arrows. A thin crack of light shone through. Even on the brightest day the room was twilit.

There was a small table with a plate of uneaten food, a flagon of water and an earthenware cup. In a corner stood a primitive wash-hand stand; on the floor two mattresses and pillows.

Gregory was leaning against the wall in the recess, staring through the narrow aperture, his only link with the outside world. He didn't turn when Roger came in. When he heard the door open he said: 'You can take it away. I don't want it.' He assumed that the visitor was the guard who brought his food.

Roger didn't know how to begin, or what to say. Despite his prejudice, he couldn't resist a sneaking admiration for Gregory's stalwart defiance of everyone who had been in contact with him.

They were of the same age, around fourteen. Roger was tall for his age and Gregory matched his height. In all other ways no two boys could have been less alike. Roger was fair, slimly built but lithe and strong. Gregory was bread shouldered and thick set. His hair was raven black; his eyes in contrast, a steely blue. Roger was sunburnt from life in the open air. Gregory was pale. From what Roger had heard about him he had led a pampered life, surrounded by obsequious servants. Roger had never had a servant. His father had brought him up to share the life of the people in the settlement. He had worked with them in the fields, hunted with them and sailed with them in their fishing boats.

But as Roger glanced at the boy lounging by the window, he could see nothing pampered about him. He looked at the broad shoulders and strong limbs in doubt. 'If it came to a fight,' he thought. 'I'm not sure that I'd get the best of it after all.'

Gregory had turned from the window. He was surprised to see a boy standing there in place of the guard that he expected. He looked Roger up and down contemptuously, as if he were a scullion from a kitchen.

'Who are you?' he demanded. 'And what are you here for?'

'I'm here because this is my room,' said Roger.

'Your room?'

'It's the room that my father set aside for me.'

'And what right has your father to put you in here with me?'

'My father is Lord Swayne.'

Gregory looked at Roger with a new interest – as if he were a curious insect dredged up from a pond.

'So, your father is Lord Swayne!' he jeered. 'For how long has he been a "lord"? He's the sort of lord the cooks make out of dough!'

He came from the window and stood by the table, legs apart, hands on hips; an imperious young nobleman putting an underling into his place.

'Your father will have a lot to answer for when my father the Earl gets here!'

It suddenly dawned upon Roger that Gregory knew nothing of what had happened since he was brought to the castle as a prisoner. Shut up in this dark room he was totally sealed off from events outside.

Roger couldn't resist getting his own back for the insults thrown at him, and he didn't mince his words. 'Your father arrived four days ago and tried to take the castle,' he told Gregory. 'Didn't you hear the fighting?'

'I heard a noise,' said Gregory, 'but couldn't see anything from this miserable slit of a window. You call this a castle! It isn't as big as my father's stables. There wasn't any fight and my father's army isn't here yet. I saw some smoke and got a nasty smell of frying bacon. It was your own men out there, cooking a meal and quarrelling over it – and you say it was a battle!'

'The smell you got wasn't bacon for a meal,' replied Roger. 'It was your men frying in the oil we poured on them. They attacked and tried to bridge the moat. Our men hit back. Yours ran for their lives and your father got the beating he deserved.'

'You're a liar,' said Gregory. 'Just a lot of silly lies.'

'If you think I'm lying,' retorted Roger, 'then I'll ask my father to have you taken down to see for yourself the burnt-out ruins of your father's bridge.'

Gregory turned his back, went to the window and stared out as if Roger wasn't there.

Remembering his father's wishes. Roger made one last attempt. 'Can't we be friends?' he asked.

'Friends?' said Gregory, 'with *you*?'

There was such withering contempt in the retort that it left no more to do or say. Roger went out, locked the door and walked back to his father's room. The old priest was there, and sat with Swayne as Roger told them what had happened.

Father Peter had seen more of Gregory than anyone, for Swayne had put the boy in his care. But he had been able to do nothing for him. He had gone to the boy's room every day but Gregory had turned his back and refused to say a word.

'He has eaten nothing,' said Father Peter. 'He's starving himself, wearing himself out.'

Swayne was sick and tired of Gregory. If the boy had behaved himself he would still have been a burden in a castle stripped for siege. If he starved himself to death, Swayne would be in duty bound to return his body to the Earl, and the Earl would declare that it had been deliberate.

He said to Roger, 'I want you to try again. It's not just a matter of making friends with a stupid, obstinate boy. We've got to keep him from starving himself to death and giving his father the chance to say we murdered him. We'll try another way. The cooks will prepare the best meal that they can manage. It will be for the two of you. You will take it in, tell him you've come to stay because it's your room as well as his, get on with your own meal and see what happens.'

The cooks resented serving their obnoxious prisoner with delicacies that he didn't deserve but they prepared a chicken with a special sauce, vegetables fresh from Father Peter's garden, honey cakes, and a small flagon of wine.

At mid-day the tray was carried up from the kitchen. A guard unpadlocked the door and Roger carried the tray in. Gregory was lying on his mattress. He looked pale and ill. His hair was dishevelled, his clothing crumpled, he looked anything but the son of a great Earl. But the pride and unbreakable spirit was still there. He turned his head and looked at Roger with a contemptuous smile.

'So it's you again?' he said. He saw the tray that Roger was carrying. 'If it's food you've got you can take it away.'

'I'm not taking it away because it's my dinner as well as yours,' replied Roger. 'This is my room and I'm staying here. If you don't want your dinner, that's fine, because there'll be all the more for me.'

Gregory didn't answer this. 'How old are you?' he said.

'Fourteen,' replied Roger.

'You don't look it,' said Gregory. 'You don't look more than a baby.'

'I'm as tall as you,' retorted Roger. 'If not taller.'

'Maybe,' said Gregory. 'But you look like a weed. Those legs of yours. They're as thin as corn stalks.'

'I bet I could race you a mile and beat you,' replied Roger.

Gregory laughed: more like a real laugh, thought Roger than anything he had heard from Gregory before.

'If we went at each other on chargers with lances,' he said, 'I'd knock you flying.'

Roger laughed back. He was beginning to enjoy it.

'We don't have chargers here,' he said, 'dressed up in gold and silver finery, or lances with blue and crimson tassels on them. We don't play at battles here. We fight them.'

Gregory laughed again. 'You can certainly answer back,' he said.

It wasn't a very edifying conversation, but it broke the ice.

The trouble with Gregory was that he had never talked to a boy of his own age in a natural way. In his father's castle he had been a little god. If he condescended to speak to the sons of the Earl's household it was an honour for them. The lesser boys were only there to bow to him and raise their caps when he went by. So it wasn't to be wondered at that his meeting with Roger had left him high and dry. His father had told him that the Swaynes were beneath contempt, a bunch of loutish 'natives'. When they captured him on the river bank it was as if a gang of ragamuffins had got hold of him, and the boy now with him was no more than the son of a ragamuffin chief.

Yet watching him from where he lay on his mattress, Gregory had to admit to himself that Roger didn't look like what his father had described the Swaynes to be. He was plainly dressed in the russet brown tunic that all the soldiers in the castle wore, but there was something about him that made Gregory wonder, for the first time in his life, whether there might not be some sort of people that had never come his way before, between the aristocracy that he belonged to and the common herd that bowed and scraped to them.

Roger put the tray on the table and laid out the dishes. There was an appetizing smell of chicken. Taking no further notice of Gregory he pulled up a stool, sat down and helped himself.

Gregory slowly got up from his mattress. He stood upright, making the most of his height, doing his best to be the commanding son of a great Earl. But he swayed from weakness and Roger saw how thin and pale he was. Much thinner than when he had strutted into the castle a week ago. His tunic hung loosely upon him, his leather belt sagged around his waist, but he had not lost his indomitable pride.

He turned his back on the table, walked to the window, and said.

'Get on with your dinner. Don't mind me.'

'Look,' said Roger, 'I'm hungry, but I'm not going to enjoy eating with you standing there. And it isn't good manners to turn your back on people.'

Gregory was stung to indignation. 'I don't have to be taught manners by you!' he shot back.

Roger tried to start his dinner but couldn't eat it with that pitiful starving boy standing by the window.

'If you go on like this you'll starve yourself to death,' he said, 'and what good are you going to be to anybody when you're dead?'

Gregory didn't answer, and there was a long silence.

Roger was desperate. He didn't want to go back to his father and say that he had failed again. He tried another way. It wasn't his usual sort of talk, but more like the language that Gregory understood.

'If you capture an enemy you treat him as he deserves. If he's fought in a dirty way, you put him in the dungeon with the rats and filth. If he's fought honourably, then you treat him honourably, as a guest. When you were captured, my father believed you to be an honourable enemy. He said I must have you in my own room and treat you as he thinks you would have treated me if I had been your captive. So why not sit down and have dinner with me?'

This did the trick: or nearly so. Gregory turned from the window, came to the table and stood over it.

'I will eat with you,' he said, 'if you understand that I am not your prisoner. You and all the rest of you in this castle are my father's prisoners, and that you'll soon find out.'

Roger let this pass. There wasn't any point in starting another argument. He got up and pulled a stool to the table opposite to him. With a smile and a bow he motioned to Gregory to join him. 'As my guest,' he said.

Gregory sat on the stool, but sideways, as if not deigning to put himself on a level with Roger by sitting squarely to him.

Roger piled a plate with chicken and vegetables and placed it before Gregory. At first Gregory pushed it about fastidiously, as he might have done in his father's hall to impress the servants. It said much for his willpower and his pride, for he must have been desperately hungry.

To ease the tension Roger began talking for all he was worth.

'We've got chickens running around in the grass behind the ramparts,' he said. 'There are cows and goats and plenty of fish in the moat. Every night we put out lines and get enough to fry for breakfast. Try these vegetables. And these oatmeal cakes. Try some of this wine. We've got six barrels of it down there in the vaults. We used to drive in to Lynn and buy it straight off the ships from Bordeaux . . .'

There wasn't any need for Roger to go on talking. Gregory had drawn his stool close to the table and was eating ravenously. Roger put some of his own helping on Gregory's plate. 'It's good,' said

Gregory, and went on eating. He ate all the honey cakes and took a drink of wine.

When he had finished he sat back and looked at Roger as if he were seeing him for the first time.

'What's your name?' he asked.

'Roger.'

'I suppose I ought to thank you,' said Gregory.

'You don't have to.'

There was a silence. It was difficult for Roger to know what to talk about. He didn't want to say anything about the siege that might send Gregory off on another of his boasting tirades about the Earl's superiority, and Gregory, full of chicken and honey cakes, was much more likeable than Roger had expected.

'Would you care to take a walk?' he asked.

'If you aren't afraid of me escaping,' said Gregory.

'I'll take your word on that.'

'I don't feel like escaping after all that dinner.'

'I must get my father's permission.'

At the door he turned and said, 'You get ready.'

'Aren't you going to lock me in again?'

'I'll risk that,' said Roger.

Swayne was delighted when Roger told him what had happened. 'It'll do him good to have some fresh air and exercise,' he said. 'Take him anywhere you like. The more he sees of the castle the better.'

When Roger got back, Gregory was washing himself at the table against the wall. Roger had brought from his father's room a small bag of his personal belongings. He lent Gregory his comb, and helped to brush down his rumpled clothes.

They went along the dark passage, down the turret steps into the main hall.

'This is where we dine at night,' said Roger.

Gregory looked around him in surprise. His father had told him that Swayne Castle was nothing better than a cow house. He saw the tapestries and coloured shields, the tables set for the evening meal, the miniature chapel in a window recess for Father Peter's evening service. It didn't fit in with what he had expected, but he couldn't let it pass without a show of bombast.

'In the hall of our castle,' he said, 'two hundred guests can sit down to supper. There's a gallery where minstrels play. At Christmas there's dancing and play actors.'

'It must be very nice,' said Roger.

They went on down the turret steps into the guardroom where men off duty were asleep. Others were playing draughts at the table. They glanced up as the two boys came in: a nod and a smile for Roger, a sidelong glance of curiosity at Gregory.

They went down the fortress steps into the surrounding grassland. Gregory was blinded by the sunlight after days in his twilit room. He shaded his eyes and screwed them up before he could look around him.

What he saw made him wonder still more. According to the Earl's officers the Swaynes were a witless bunch of farmhands and fishermen who happened to have a ramshackle old castle on their land into which they would run and hide when they heard that the Earl was coming. They had, it was said, no trained soldiers; no idea of organizing a military defence.

It didn't take Gregory long to see that his people had got things wrong. It was true that there was nothing military about the scene around him: no array of war machines or warlike soldiers in helmets and chain armour. But all the men he saw were orderly and disciplined, dressed alike in plain russet brown, like Roger. It looked, in fact, more like a small, well-ordered farm.

Cows were grazing placidly on the thick green pasture. A man was feeding pigs in a sty from a sack of acorns: and a cockerel was chasing hens around in an enclosure. Some men off duty were playing a game of quoits: throwing rope rings at an upright stake. Others were practising bowmanship; a few were just lazing in the sun.

'You tell me,' said Gregory, 'that my father's army has arrived.'

'He's been here a week,' said Roger. 'And we've had two battles.'

Gregory said nothing. The whole thing just didn't make sense.

Roger took him on to the ramparts and they walked the whole

way round. Some men were working at the gatehouse, repairing the broken doors and clearing the remaining wreckage of the Earl's shattered bridge and penthouses. Roger said nothing about it to Gregory as they went by.

They came to the stretch of ramparts that faced across the meadows to the Earl's pavilion on the hill crest.

'Your father's headquarters,' said Roger. 'Very grand.'

It was so close that if they had lowered the drawbridge Gregory could have walked there in ten minutes. Roger expected him to show some feeling about it, but he was quite casual and dispassionate.

'Looks all right from here,' he said. 'But it's sweltering on a hot day, and at night when they light the lamps it gets full of moths and cockroaches. I've slept in it, and I know.'

Gregory's lack of interest in his father's whereabouts puzzled Roger. 'The Earl would pay a big ransom for you if we agreed to send you back,' he said.

It astonished Roger when Gregory laughed and said, 'My father wouldn't pay a penny for me.'

He had evidently let fall more than he intended, for he corrected himself and was back on his high horse again.

'You wouldn't understand these things,' he said. 'Ransom money is a confession of defeat. You pay it to get somebody back when you can't do it by force of arms. My father knows very well that he'll have me back all right when he's ready to throw his army against this castle.'

It didn't sound convincing but Roger let it pass. He was beginning to like Gregory in a mixed-up sort of way. He was irritating when he got bombastic, but when he came down to earth, he was a good companion. Roger took him to the watch tower on the summit of the fortress from where they could see the deserted town, and the harbour, and a wide view of the surrounding country.

When they got back to their room Father Peter was there with a chess board and a box of chessmen. 'Do you play chess?' he asked Gregory.

'I like it,' said Gregory.

'Then you and Roger can fight out your battles on your own,' said Father Peter.

It wasn't easy for Roger to go down to the hall for his evening meal, leaving Gregory locked up as a prisoner, so the cooks prepared a tray for the two of them and they had the meal together.

Afterwards they played chess until it was too dark to see, then stretched out on their mattresses.

Sitting face to face with Roger at their meal, Gregory had been stiff and formal, determined to keep familiarity at a distance, but lying there in the darkness, with Roger on his mattress against the opposite wall, he began to relax and talk more naturally, and Roger was able to piece together the strange, mixed-up affair that Gregory's life had been.

The Earl, always out for the best, had made a great catch when he married a daughter of the ruling house of France. As things were in those days, the women of high estate were usually more cultured, more intelligent and better educated than the men. The Earl was bred for war and martial exercises, for the tough business of managing large estates and keeping on good terms with the King. His wife was often left alone, and gave herself to the gentle arts of reading, poetry and music.

So it came about that when the Earl was away, Gregory had been under his mother's influence. She read history to him; recited the poetic legends; taught him to enjoy music. She gave him a good tutor who taught him to write lucidly and read the classics. She taught him to carve and model, to paint and illustrate.

But his father had no use for all this arty stuff. He wanted his son to grow up like himself, not into an effeminate poet. He set about knocking the rubbish out of him. He took him hunting, taught him jousting, paraded him in magnificent clothes at Royal Assemblies, told him, in fact, to be a man.

Gregory had been torn between the two. He had something both of his father and his mother in him. He enjoyed the strenuous hunting days and the flamboyant parades so dear to the Earl, but he couldn't see why he shouldn't also enjoy the arts and the culture that his mother had implanted in him.

The Earl, being the possessive type, resented this, and was always out to knock Gregory into the shape that he considered proper. But Gregory, having a mind of his own, dug his heels in and stood his ground. He was sometimes rebellious, and gave his father plenty in return. The Earl, in disgust, had turned to his younger son, who was much more compliant and obedient, and promised to become a mirror of his father.

There was no doubt a good deal more to it than appeared on the surface when Gregory had said that his father 'wouldn't give a penny for him' in ransom. Roger only gleaned fragments of this as the two boys lay talking in the darkness. But long after Gregory had gone to sleep, Roger lay pondering about him.

'He's a queer sort of fellow,' he thought. 'First he brags about what great warriors his family have always been, and how they're going to knock the stuffing out of us. Then he recites a poem about a Greek god who turned a princess into a rainbow. Anyway, he's not nearly as bad as I thought he was. I might even get to like him.'

Chapter Seven

One morning a contingent of mercenaries arrived in the Earl's camp to replace the men lost in the battle at the gatehouse. Their leader was a young German named Conrad. He was more an engineer than a soldier, and had made a name for himself on the Continent as the designer of powerful siege weapons. They spent the afternoon surveying the castle from every point of view, and in the evening went to dine with the Earl in his pavilion.

The Earl soon got impatient when they began to talk in technical terms about weapons for bombardment. Why not a direct assault upon the ramparts? Surely a well-trained company of three hundred mercenaries, with ladders to bridge the moat and scale the walls could easily overwhelm a garrison of amateurs who could scarcely number more than fifty?

Raymond and Conrad came back with a good answer.

The castle, they said, although small, was well sited for defence. It stood on a natural plateau with low-lying fields around it, and the ramparts on all sides dropped sheer to a broad moat. The moat and the ramparts presented a formidable double barrier, side by side.

They also reminded the Earl that the approaches to the castle, from every side, had been cleared of cover to the width of about 300 yards, exposed to the arrows of the defenders.

'Then why not a night assault?' retorted the Earl. 'You can attack in the darkness and be on to them before they can see you. And they won't stand a chance at close quarters with your men.'

Raymond and Conrad had a good answer to that too. Night fighting was notoriously hazardous under the best conditions. To attack the unbroken ramparts of a castle with no knowledge of what lay beyond would be suicidal in the darkness.

'The defenders would have the supreme advantage of knowing their ground,' said Raymond. 'The attackers would be like men blindfold. Having scaled the walls they would need to organize a concerted assault upon the garrison. They would be lost in the darkness, surrounded by defenders who know every inch of the ground.'

The Earl began to lose his temper.

'You assured me,' he said to Raymond, 'that when you were up to strength with these replacements you would take the castle without the least delay!'

'We can,' answered Raymond, 'with the help of your levies. If my men were to advance across open land, loaded with ladders to bridge the moat and scale the walls, the survivors would be too few for the final assault. But if your own men carry the ladders to the moat and lay them across, my mercenaries will follow up and do the rest.'

He had touched the Earl on a delicate spot, as he intended. He knew quite well that the Earl could never persuade his levies to pave the way. The mercenaries had been employed to do the dirty work; the Earl's own men were to come in when the fighting was over and grab the plunder.

To do them justice Raymond and Conrad weren't merely trying to spin out the siege for what they could collect in wages.

Raymond could not afford to risk his reputation in another disaster, and the sort of attack demanded by the Earl was asking for it. The castle was a hard nut to crack, and he wasn't taking any chances.

Conrad assured the Earl that once the siege machines were installed he could guarantee victory in a week. 'We cannot penetrate the skin of this castle,' he said, 'but we can destroy its heart.'

The Earl could do nothing but accept. It meant delay and more money spent on costly siege machines, but at least he had the guarantee that once these weapons were in operation, victory would be swift and overwhelming.

The garrison was puzzled by the enemy's inaction. With such a massive army at his command they expected the Earl to waste no time in staging new and even fiercer assaults upon the ramparts. But as the days went by and nothing happened they began to believe that the Earl had accepted defeat and would soon pack up to go.

Swayne and his officers didn't allow such wishful thinking to relax their vigilance, but it seemed as if the Earl's army had lost all interest in the siege. The sentries continued their monotonous patrol between the guard tents but away off in the main encampment all they could see were men fishing in the river, chopping wood, or hanging clothes and blankets out to air.

Life in the castle was pleasant in that peaceful interlude. The spirits of the garrison were high. The victory at the gatehouse and successful reinforcement had given them assurance that they could beat their assailants any time they got within fighting distance of them.

It was hot and stuffy in the fortress on those late summer days and the men off duty slept in the open air. There was target practice to keep the muscles trim for bows. Wrestling was good for active men confined behind castle walls.

The evening meal was laid on with ceremony to keep the men up to scratch. Afterwards there was music on home-made instruments that men had brought with them to the castle: fiddles and reed pipes and horns and harps. The rest sang in chorus. For most of the garrison, young and impressionable, accustomed to farm cottages and fishing huts, there was romance and glamour on those evenings in the lamplit hall.

After three weeks with no move from the enemy the certainty grew that the Earl had shot his bolt and was only delaying his departure to save his face. Every morning they expected to see the tents being struck, and wagons being loaded up to go. It was only a matter of days, they reckoned, before they would be free to get back to their farms and fishing boats.

It therefore came with all the more surprise when one dark night strange noises were heard close to the ramparts. The officer on watch sent word to Swayne, who came on to the ramparts to listen.

It wasn't a noise he could put a name to. The creaking of truck wheels was followed by the clatter of tools thrown down. A man with a guttural voice was giving orders. Sometimes there was the clang of a spade against a stone. There was a drone of talk. Somebody had a cough. Occasionally there was a laugh.

There was no point in calling an alert. Whatever they were doing out there in the dark couldn't be a prelude to a surprise attack. There was too much talk and noise. Swayne told the sentries to relax and stayed out with them for the remainder of the night.

Before dawn the noises stopped. They heard tools being thrown into a truck and the creak of wheels as the truck was driven away. Straining their eyes through the twilight the sentries could see a white blur in the field. As the light grew stronger they saw that the mysterious workers had dug out a circle of turf down to the underlying chalk and piled the turf around it as a bulwark.

It was clearly the beginning of some sort of emplacement. What troubled Swayne was its nearness to the castle ramparts: barely fifty yards from the far side of the moat. His officers suggested certain possibilities. Maybe it was the start of a tunnel to burrow under the moat and come up inside the castle: or a deep culvert to pierce the moat and drain the water off into the surrounding fields. It could be, for all they knew. It could be anything. If, as Swayne suspected, it was an emplacement to take a machine for bombardment, he saw little serious danger in it. The ramparts were banked with solid earth and the walls of the central fortress were too thick and strong for the heaviest missiles to damage them.

That first digging party was a scratch on the surface of a massive undertaking that grew in volume night by night. As soon as it was dark the silent fields around the castle seethed with life; wagons creaking, the clatter of unloading, the gleam of lanterns and the drone of voices. Before dawn the sounds would die away, and when the sun rose the fields were deserted save for the sentries at the guard tents, moving to and fro on their monotonous patrol.

But at every dawn the garrison could see that the work was increasing as more and more workmen were brought in. Two big emplacements were taking shape on opposite sides of the castle with a dozen small ones spaced evenly between.

If the Earl had been aiming at a war of nerves he could scarcely have done better. The high spirits of the garrison were draining away, turning them into angry, sullen men. What angered them was their impotence to hit back. The emplacements were within easy range of the ramparts and they wanted to harass the workers with arrows and missiles from their catapults. Swayne refused to let them shoot blind into the night: a waste of arrows needed for better targets. Small missiles from their catapults would do no harm to the massive emplacements and merely arouse derision among the enemy.

What hurt most was the disillusionment. The long silence of the enemy had convinced them that the Earl had resigned himself to failure and would soon back up and go. They had begun to talk confidently of soon returning to their families, but now found themselves surrounded by earth-works ominous and menacing.

The enemy began to dig communication trenches from the emplacements to positions well behind, enabling the workmen to come and go by daylight, secure and unseen by the sentries on the ramparts.

Swayne did what he could to keep up the spirits of his men. He got them together and talked to them every day. 'It's clear enough that they are planning to bombard us,' he said, 'but they can shoot a thousand missiles at us and be no nearer to capturing the castle. They can't knock down the ramparts or destroy the moat. No missile can do more than scratch the fortress and the sentries will be safe in the rampart turrets. If the Earl thinks he can beat us by shooting rocks at us he'll have to think again.'

Dinner was served at night with the same lustre, with music afterwards, and singing. The men tried to rise to it, but the heart had gone out of them. The strain and suspense of waiting was nagging at their nerves.

The enemy preparations now took a new turn. The digging was finished and mule-drawn wagons arrived with loads of heavy scaffolding. It was carried up the trenches into the emplacements and hammering began. Two massive posts were installed inside the large emplacements, with crossbeams overhead. Consignments of materials included coils of thick rope and bars of iron, cogged wheels, and heavy sacks of ballast. Braziers were lit and welding began. The garrison could hear the ring of sledgehammers against iron. The smoke from the braziers drifted across the moat and over the ramparts.

At last the days of waiting ended. One morning a party of mercenaries came marching across the fields and disappeared into the trench that led to one of the big emplacements. The Earl came out of his pavilion and stood talking to some officers. Presently two servants came out of his pavilion carrying a big chair. The Earl took his seat in it, like a Roman emperor awaiting a barbaric entertainment.

The garrison could hear work going on in the emplacement: the grinding of winches: the clang of a hammer. Then a curious object appeared in view above the bulwark of the emplacement. It looked like a heavy sack of ballast fastened to the end of a pivot. It came up very slowly, to the grinding of the winches.

The next thing happened so suddenly and violently that even the garrison, ready for anything, were astonished.

On a word of command the loaded pivot was released. As it plunged out of sight a long shooting arm sprang up behind it, fitted with a holder containing some sort of missile. It hit the crossbeam a resounding blow: the missile was projected with tremendous force and came hurtling towards the castle. The garrison saw a dark object flying overhead. It soared over the summit of the fortress with yards to spare and landed with a thud that frightened some pigeons in the field beyond the castle.

Suspense released, the garrison raised a derisive cheer and roared with laughter. So this was the Earl's new weapon, after all those weeks of preparation! He didn't even kill a pigeon for his supper!

Nothing happened for half an hour. A lot more work went on in the emplacement. An officer was giving orders. Then they heard the winches creaking and saw the load of ballast rise once more above the bulwarks of the emplacement.

At a word of command the cables were released and the load of ballast went crashing down. The missile arm came springing up and hit the crossbeam another resounding blow.

The second shot, to the delight of the garrison, was more futile than the first. The missile went off sideways and landed close to one of the enemy's own guard tents. The garrison doubled up with laughter when they saw the sentries running for their lives with the missile bounding along the ground behind them. It was glorious fun. They waited with relish for the next shot, hoping it would go off backwards and knock the Earl's pavilion down.

But that was the end of it for the day. Soon afterwards they saw the mercenaries come out of the communication trench and return to camp.

Release from those long days of suspense reacted upon the garrison like magic. They had never been so happy: so confident of victory. The Earl's fearsome machine was a ridiculous fiasco. At dinner that night a man with a flair for songs began inventing rhyming couplets pouring scorn upon the Earl's preposterous invention, and the others joined lustily in the chorus.

Swayne let them have their fun. After what they had been through they deserved it. But he knew that the man who had conceived that massive array of emplacements would not discard them because a couple of shots had gone astray.

But on one thing his mind was now at rest. He had feared that those ominous preparations might be the prelude to some new form of attack: flame throwers, possibly to saturate the castle with smoke and fumes to make life insufferable, but from what he had seen that day he was satisfied that the engines were designed to throw projectiles with nothing new about them: to intimidate and to destroy anything hit by chance that was easily destructible, but nothing more. It would need an earth-quake to destroy the ramparts and the fortress. If the Earl shot missiles from all his emplacements the garrison could take safe cover.

On his way to his room on the summit of the fortress Swayne went in to say goodnight to Gregory and Roger. The two boys were lying on the floor playing a game they had invented with the chessmen.

'What's all this?' asked Swayne.

'We're fighting for the castle,' said Roger. 'The white chessmen are our men; the black ones the enemy.'

Swayne was surprised to see Gregory so cheerful. He had expected him to be angry and humiliated by the fiasco of the Earl's machine that day. 'Who's winning the battle on the floor?' he asked.

'I am,' said Gregory. 'My father made a mess of it out there today but if I had been in command I'd have taken this castle long ago.'

'In that case,' said Swayne, 'It's lucky we've got you where you are.'

The Earl had returned to his pavilion livid with fury. The garrison had settled down to a joyful supper. The only reflective man that evening was Conrad, the young German engineer.

Long after his men had left the emplacement he remained there alone with the machine of his invention, pondering over it: testing its structure and alignment.

In siege parlance it was called a 'trebuchet'. Conrad had seen them in operation on the Continent: clumsy hit-or-miss affairs, more spectacular than destructive. He was convinced that given form and precision they could be devastating.

His employment at Swayne Castle had given him a godsent opportunity: a free hand, money to spend, all the men he needed for the labour.

The Earl had quibbled about the cost and the waste of time, but Conrad's promise to destroy the castle in a matter of days had paved the way, and everything he needed had been forthcoming. It made it the more galling that faults had shown themselves.

He began a careful reassessment of his work. He checked the standing of the structure. He measured the shooting arm and made corrections in its alignment. He examined the cup that held the missile, and the apparatus that held the secret of his ranging.

He was checking the alignment of the shooting arm when a messenger came hurrying down the communication trench.

'The Earl wants to see you,' he announced.

'When I'm ready,' said Conrad, and went on calmly with his work. He was very tired, but the worst part of the day was still ahead, when he faced the angry Earl.

The Earl had reason to be angry. When Conrad had explained his master plan, the cost had been appalling. The hardest oak was needed for the framework of his machines, and a dozen woodcutters were employed to fell and shape the timber. The shooting arms had to be reinforced with iron: the cups for the missiles specially forged. Rope for the winches must be the strongest obtainable. Even the missiles for the two big trebuchets had to be tooled to precision dimensions.

Expert craftsmen were brought in from Norwich. It cost money, and more money, and time as well as money. The Earl had fumed with impatience at the slowness of the work while the cost of his great army was eating away his fortune.

His only consolation had been Conrad's positive assurance that once his battery of siege machines went into action the destruction of the castle would only be the matter of a few days.

So when he was told that the first machine would be at work that afternoon the Earl had naturally expected immediate and shattering results. He had had his chair placed outside his pavilion and settled down to enjoy the sight of the castle being smashed to pieces.

And now this ridiculous fiasco. Two shots in the whole afternoon. Neither had even touched the castle. They had frightened a few pigeons and sent the garrison into roars of laughter. It was enough to make him sick.

Raymond was in the pavilion when Conrad arrived. The Earl was striding up and down, purple in the face, almost inarticulate with rage.

'So here you are!' he shouted. 'I spent a small fortune on what you wanted because I thought you knew your business! And all you do is to make me a laughing stock, not only with the enemy, but with my own army! I'll have no elaborate excuses! I want to know plainly what went wrong.'

Conrad never turned a hair. 'Wrong?' he said. 'Nothing went wrong.'

The Earl nearly exploded. 'Are you telling me,' he shouted, 'that all these costly machines can do is what I saw this afternoon!'

Conrad spoke as if explaining to a child. 'The missiles this afternoon were testing shots,' he said. 'These complicated weapons need careful setting and adjustment. Nobody can expect perfection without trial. Today I gained valuable information that I will explain to you.'

He unrolled his notes and spread them on the table.

'The first shot went high,' he said, 'because the shooting arm was a fraction too close to the crossbeam. The second went wide because the impact of the first had moved the crossbeam slightly out of true. I must strengthen the foundations of these crossbeams. The cups for the missiles must be padded to prevent them from rotating in flight. A spinning missile has no penetration.'

All this meant nothing to the Earl. He wanted results: not figures and calculations.

'I can only assume that you know what you are talking about,' he said, 'but what, in plain words, does it mean?'

'Simply that there is nothing basically wrong,' replied Conrad. 'Nothing that I cannot put right as a result of the tests today.'

'But all this will take time?'

'Less time,' said Conrad, 'than if I had installed the other machines before trying out this first one.'

'But how long?' demanded the Earl.

'In about three weeks,' replied Conrad. 'I think we shall be ready. And then you will see things happen that will gladden your heart.'

Chapter Eight

The Earl had provided the garrison with a guessing game, and any guess was as good as the next.

When the days went by and nothing happened the optimists believed that the fiasco with the siege machine had convinced the Earl that he was beaten and would soon pack up and go. It looked as if they were right when they saw a company of about a hundred men march out of the camp one morning and take the road for home. They weren't to know that it was merely a detachment of redundant levies released to return for the harvests, but they reckoned at the time that it was the beginning of a complete disbandment, and their view was strengthened when some workmen came along to dismantle the big siege engine and carry the stuff away.

But there were others who couldn't believe that the Earl had tamely surrendered, and they were soon proved to be right, for a few days later the workmen returned to rebuild the siege engine with new equipment and work began again in all the emplacements around the castle.

It didn't upset the garrison. If the Earl wanted to have another fling, then let him. They had the assurance of their Commander that if the Earl shot hundreds of missiles at the castle he could never knock the ramparts down or destroy the moat, and the iron-hard walls of the fortress were impervious. So they watched the new activities without concern, only hoping that the Earl would get on with it and make the final impotent attack that would get him nowhere and send him home. In the meantime they enjoyed the lingering days of summer. Secure from surprise attack they kept in the open, and the young ones took a moonlight swim around the moat.

It happened one evening when the garrison was at dinner in the hall.

The tables had been cleared and the men who played instruments were preparing to begin when a sudden crunching impact sent a shudder through the fortress. A shower of dust and debris from the rafters smothered the tables. A pile of dishes on a sideboard clattered down and a lamp fell from its bracket on the wall.

It came so unexpectedly, so unlike anything they associated with a falling missile, that the first thought was of a violent buffet from a gale of wind. Thunder had been rumbling in the distance. It could have been the beginning of a freak storm. But the tremor through the fortress had scarcely gone before there came a second impact, as violent as the first: this time on the opposite side of the fortress. They heard masonry falling: thudding on the ground outside. Swayne sent the men to their sleeping quarters, and with one of his officers went out to investigate. It was a dark night with a drizzle of rain. They could see little of the wall above them but found some fragments of broken masonry on either side of the fortress where the missiles had struck.

They walked around the ramparts, questioning the sentries. They were surprised to hear that missiles had come over, but one man said he heard a 'rushing noise' and put it down to a gust of wind.

The lanterns remained glowing in the emplacements, but there was nothing more that night. Swayne kept watch with the sentries on the ramparts until it was light enough to see what damage had been done.

Both missiles had struck the fortress about midway up its height and both had torn a jagged hole about a foot wide. Judging by the debris they had penetrated deeply, but were far from breaking through the yard-thick walls.

Yet for Swayne those two shots were a great deal more ominous than the relatively small damage done.

There was something here that changed his whole conception of what lay ahead. A siege machine, as he had understood it, needed to throw its missile high into the air in order to hit its target at long range. Swayne had reckoned that for a missile to come far enough to hit the fortress it would be falling at the time, with no power in it beyond its weight. It would be deflected by the wall and barely scratch it.

But these had left far more than a scratch. They had churned jagged holes that only a missile head on, at full force, could have made.

He was shocked by their precision. It could scarcely have been a fluke that two missiles, shot from opposite sides, could hit the fortress walls at exactly the same height.

He searched among the fallen debris for the missiles. Finding none, he assumed that they had been shattered by the impact, and then a man called out for him to come and look at something lying in the grass.

It lay about twenty yards away: a ball of brownish stone: not much larger than a man's clenched fist. It was expertly tooled and immensely heavy. Swayne recognized it as granite, and it showed no sign of its tremendous impact against the fortress wall. It lay there unscarred: clearly much harder than the stone that it had shattered and brought down.

Conrad evidently believed in playing upon his adversary's nerves. Having delivered his first two missiles in the evening twilight to give the garrison a sleepless night, he couldn't have timed his next shots better, for Swayne had barely realized the significance of those deadly granite missiles when he heard the sharp impact of the shooting arm in the emplacement as it struck the crossbeam above the trebuchet.

The missile hit the fortress with a resounding crash. Splintered stone shot out in all directions and when the cloud of powdered mortar had subsided there was another jagged hole in the fortress wall. Within a few seconds the trebuchet on the opposite side of the fortress let fly. Another crash; another shower of broken stone and dust; another ugly, jagged wound.

Swayne wasn't easily rattled. He had won the trust of the garrison through calmness and resource. In every emergency he had foreseen the dangers and produced an answer to them. This time he had no answer. He had totally underestimated the power of these machines and their deadly accuracy.

The enemy's plan was clear. They were concentrating upon the most vulnerable part of the fortress where a structure of heavy oak beams formed the roofing of the hall and gave support to the upper floors. The beams were built into the walls: strong enough to withstand any strain that the builders had foreseen. But if missiles went on hitting with the same force and precision the walls would be so weakened that the collapse of a beam would bring the whole structure down in ruins, burying beneath it the vital well of fresh water and food reserves stored in the vaults. Conrad had told the Earl that the attack was to destroy the castle's heart, and that was what he had now begun: precisely and deliberately.

Swayne's officers were standing by: waiting for his orders. He knew what was in their minds. He had assured them time and again that no missile could possibly do serious damage to the fortress, and now they were destroying it, stone by stone.

Searching desperately in his mind for a possible answer he recalled an old legend he had heard in his boyhood. When Duke William of Normandy was besieging the castle of a rebellious baron the garrison hung cowhides over the walls and shouted in derision, 'Hides for the tanner's son!' It was an insult to the bastard Duke, whose mother came from a family of tanners, but might not there have been a more practical purpose?

When the cattle had been slaughtered to provision the castle the hides had been cleaned and stored for coverings to beds and embrasures in the event of a hard winter of siege. It was a forlorn gamble, but better than having the men standing helplessly around.

'Get the stuff out of store,' he said to his officers. 'Bring hay from the fodder sheds. Collect all the ropes we've got, all the sacking and straps and canvas.'

There was no time to explain what he had in mind, which was probably all to the good. Had the officers known his intention they would probably have thought he had lost his reason. But they asked no questions and went to it with a will.

The hides and hog skins were stacked in an outbuilding some distance from the fortress, and the men could work beyond danger of the missiles concentrated on the fortress walls.

The hides were stretched out on the ground: fodder was heaped on them: rolled up into bolsters and tied with rope.

They began to get the measure of the bombardment. It took the enemy about ten minutes to draw back the shooting arms of the trebuchets, reload and shoot again. When a volley had come over the men took advantage of that interlude of safety to drag some of the bolsters to the fortress. A team was waiting inside to drag the unwieldy bolsters up the narrow, winding steps to the summit of the fortress where others were waiting to lash them together like strings of giant sausages.

It was a desperate race against time. The enemy tactics were to deliver double punches. After the interval for reloading both trebuchets let fly almost together: the second missile driving home its blow while the fortress still quivered from the first. The debris had scarcely fallen from a new wound on the front of the fortress when the blow on the back wall forced another shower of loosened stone from it.

There was soon a cluster of deep wounds on both sides of the fortress, so close together that when the missiles began widening the cavities whole segments of the wall would collapse. Swayne knew that in a few hours, at the present rate of destruction, the enemy's work would be done.

The men working in the open, stuffing and lashing the bolsters, were in relative freedom. For those inside the fortress, lugging the bolsters up the steps, the double impacts of the missiles came like a blow between the eyes. Within the enclosed fortress they echoed like a clap of thunder: the fortress quivered: stones and debris, shaken from the inner walls and ceilings, came thudding down the turret steps: the dust well-nigh choked and blinded them.

At last sufficient bolsters had been dragged up to the summit to cover one of the ravaged walls, and during a spell between the volleys they were lowered, roped together and lashed to the ramparts above.

The work was barely finished when they heard the impact of the shooting arm of the trebuchet against the crossbeam and the whine of the next missile. It struck full force against the padding. Instead of the violent crash and shattering of stone there was a muffled thud. The missile buried itself in the thick stuffing of a cowhide and dropped to the ground like a swatted wasp.

Swayne's men were astonished. None more so than Swayne himself. He had expected little from the valiant labours of his men. It needed proof to show that a well-stuffed bolster that gave to the punch was far more resistant than a rigid wall of stone. Cheered by their success the garrison redoubled their labours to cover the opposite wall. When the job was finished the fortress looked like a giant with a huge padded leather jacket covering his chest and back.

The garrison was exultant. They had beaten the Earl at another of his games. They now waited with relish, instead of dread, for each new volley to arrive, and cheered as the missiles buried themselves in the padding and had their deadly sting drawn out of them.

Swayne saw it less as a triumph than as a precarious reprieve. How long the bolsters could withstand those murderous missiles he couldn't tell.

About mid-day Conrad opened up with the catapults installed in the smaller emplacements around the castle.

These, known as mangonels, were simple in design. A plank of willow, oiled to increase its spring, was bolted upright in a clamp and drawn back with a rope. A missile was inserted in a cap, and on release the plank sprang back and sent the missile flying.

With all his careful planning, Conrad had opened up with the mangonels too late. He had no doubt reckoned that after four hours of merciless bombardment from the trebuchets the fortress would be so ruined that the garrison would be driven out into the open to be bombarded with a storm of missiles from the catapults.

He had missed his chance. If the catapult shots had rained down on the garrison working in the open, they could never have prepared the bolsters to protect the fortress walls. As it was they had practically finished when the first volley came over.

Swayne ordered his men to take cover inside the fortress and from the watch tower on the summit he saw what havoc there would have been if the working parties had been caught outside.

The catapult missiles had no destructive power against stone walls and that was not intended. They were designed to intimidate, and make work impossible outside. They were shot high into the air and came down vertically like bolts from the blue. Unlike the ponderous trebuchets they could reload in a couple of minutes, and a dozen of them working around the ramparts could keep up a ceaseless bombardment.

Swayne's men, knowing that they had been the intended victims, enjoyed the catapult bombardment as a fascinating spectacle. They were safe enough: out of range, on the summit of the fortress, but could see the mangonels at work around them. They shot in turns, in clockwise order. By the time the whole battery had sent its missiles flying the first was ready to shoot again. And so a steady pelt came down in the land around the fortress. They were, apparently, small boulders from the beach, light enough for the catapults, but judging by the thud they made when they hit the ground, heavy enough to crush a man's skull.

Swayne took stock of the situation, as it was after nearly a day of intense attack.

He could claim that the castle had won the first round. The bolsters were taking the strain of their beating. The masons reported no serious damage to the interior of the fortress. None of the missiles had penetrated beyond about a foot, and the walls were three times that depth. The missiles were concentrated upon a circumscribed target on two sides of the fortress, now covered by the bolsters. So long as the bolsters survived, the walls were safe, for the trebuchets were fixed weapons, and couldn't be moved around. Their purpose was to gnaw through the walls by persistent impact upon two vital areas, and that, for the time being, had been frustrated by the padding.

The catapults were a different problem. They had no specific target and the shots were falling all around the open area between the fortress and the ramparts. A lot of work had to be done out there. The livestock had to be cared for in the sheds: the sentries in the rampart turrets had to be relieved: wood had to be brought in to cook the food, and the garrison, cooped up in the stagnant atmosphere of the fortress, would suffer from lack of fresh air and exercise. Everything depended upon how long the Earl could keep it up, and it looked as if he could go on for days, and weeks, if necessary. The garrison had no means of hitting back.

Swayne called the men together in the hall. After a day of endless labour they were deady tired; their hands torn and bleeding from wrenching at the bolsters. He said what he could to reassure them. So far they had got the upper hand. By bolstering the fortress walls, he said, they had saved the fortress from destruction. 'The Earl no doubt reckoned he would have won by now, but he's no nearer tonight than when he started.'

He had the men served with a good measure of wine and told them to get some rest.

All night they heard the muffled thud of the granite balls hitting the buffers on the fortress but towards dawn there sometimes came the crash of a missile and the sound of falling stone as one struck the naked wall.

At dawn they found that the missiles had cut through some of the ropes that held the bolsters and the ground below was strewn with them.

They began collecting them and dragging them back into the fortress. It had rained in the night. The bolsters were sodden and heavy to lug up the narrow winding steps. At the summit they were repaired and hung again to cover the gaps laid bare.

It was an endless, straining job. As soon as one gap was repaired a missile would bring down another string of buffers and the work began again.

For some hours the garrison held their own. Few missiles hit the naked walls, but it was a perilous job out there in the open, dragging the bolsters in. The men were exposed to the ceaseless shots from the catapults. They got some protection by having a watchman who could call a warning if any threatened to fall close by and the men had time to avoid them.

Towards evening Swayne knew that they were fighting a losing battle. The ropes holding the bolsters were fraying and wearing out. Many of the hides were tearing open, strewing the ground with their stuffing when they fell.

Risking the shots from the catapults some men made a run for the gatehouse to cut away the thick cables that worked the drawbridge and to get the chains from the portcullis. Safe back, the chains and cables took the place of the worn-out ropes, and the torn and battered bolsters took the strain.

By nightfall Swayne knew that the wrenching labour and sleepless nights were dragging the men towards the limits of endurance. Another night of merciless bombardment would drain them of all resolution that remained. He had to do something to break the strain, even if it was a shameless piece of make-believe.

He went to the kitchen and talked with the cooks. What sort of meal could they serve for a special occasion? The men had done valiant work and deserved a reward. The cooks rose to it. One braved the bombardment to run to the poultry house and return with half a dozen chickens. Father Peter went to the storeroom for some of the delicacies hoarded there: honey and preserved fruit in jars: cinnamon and ginger. Flasks were filled from the barrels in the vaults.

Swayne sent round word that dinner would be served that evening in the hall. The garrison couldn't believe it. For two days they had lived on scraped up food, crouched in the dark guardroom. The hall was a shambles of dust and debris shaken down by the bombardment. Swayne had it swept clear: lanterns were lit around the walls: a log fire was set blazing and the cooks laid the tables as if for a festive dinner.

The garrison came in, still mystified, and what happened next must have made them believe they were dreaming the scene of a past evening before the ordeal began.

Swayne came in with Father Peter and the two boys: Swayne in his blue cloak, silver clasp at the shoulder, engraved with the Swayne crest, Father Peter immaculate in his priestly robes. The only thing to tell the men they weren't dreaming was Roger's black eye, for Roger had come near being blinded that afternoon by a splinter of stone when he was helping to bring in some fallen buffers. But even Roger, despite his painful bruise, had spruced himself up, washed his face and brushed his hair, and looked as if he were arriving at a Royal reception.

The unsung hero of the evening was Father Peter. As the old priest went to the little chapel in the alcove to say grace in his spotless white priestly robes nobody would have guessed that after dark he had gone out in his old patched linen tunic and braved the missiles to gather an armful of watercress from the moat side. But there, miraculously, were the bowls of cress along the table

When grace was over it was usual for the men to relax and talk, but now the tired, nerve-racked men could not relax.

'Pass the wine round,' Swayne said, 'take a drink. 'There are a few things I want to say, and then we'll get down to the food.'

The flagons were passed along the tables. The men took a drink and colour began to return to their drawn, haggard faces. The wine began to do its work. There was a booming thud against the wall outside; the lights in the oil lamps dipped and a tremor ran through the hall.

'The Earl seems to know we're having a party, and is knocking to come in,' said Swayne, 'but if he thinks he can disturb us, he's wasting his time.'

The men laughed: the first laugh that had come to the fortress since the ordeal began. The Earl couldn't have helped Swayne better than with that missile. It paved the way for him, and he stood up to speak while the men were still laughing.

'You may think it too soon to celebrate a victory,' he said, 'You'll wonder how I can talk about victory when we're still under siege, and having to put up with this bombardment. But what we have done in these past two days has made final victory certain. When the Earl let fly with his siege weapons he believed he'd knock this fortress into ruins by now. And that he would have done if you hadn't given it a padded jacket. We've got the measure of it now. It's hard work, but if we go on replacing the fallen buffers to keep the walls protected, the Earl can bang his head against them till the crack of doom, and won't destroy them.

'You'll ask how long he can keep it up? The answer is that he's got a thousand men out there and he's got to pay them every day. He's rich, but his money isn't going to last for ever. You've seen those granite balls he's shooting at us. They have to be tooled to a perfect shape. Each one is a full day's work for a mason, and masons charge a lot of money. So every time a missile buries itself in those buffers outside you can say to yourself: "Bang goes another day's pay for a mason."

'So you see it's a battle between the Earl's money, and your resolution to hold on. The day the Earl's money runs out, he's finished, because his men work for money and nothing else. And judging by the way you've beaten him so far I'm sure that your supply of resolution is going to outlast the Earl's supply of money.

'And now,' he said, 'let's enjoy our dinner.'

It was, as Swayne well knew, a shameless piece of bluff, but as a 'pep talk' it worked wonders.

The wine was passed round again. The men were exultant. Their leader never promised anything that could not be fulfilled, and they trusted every word of it. When another missile shook the fortress one of them shouted out, 'Another day's pay gone for a mason!'

The chicken stew was excellent. If more missiles hit the fortress they weren't even heard, for the men were singing uproariously.

'I am afraid they are a little drunk,' said Father Peter, 'but I must confess that I am rather drunk myself.'

The 'pep talk' broke the strain and cheered the men up, but they woke to another bleak dawn with the ground strewn with holsters shot down in the night and the bombardment more ferocious than ever.

Many of the bolsters were shattered beyond repair. Everything that could protect the walls was used to fill the gaps; the sleeping mattresses and pillows: the tapestries from the hall: old sacks were stuffed with the straw from the split bolsters. The table tops were taken from their trestles and hung down. They strung down the logs for the kitchen fires and braved the missiles in a run to the gatehouse to collect the rafts they had built to carry their wounded men over the moat. The strong cables and chains from the gatehouse stood firm and by the end of the third day the garrison had just held their own. From a hundred granite missiles barely a dozen had struck the naked walls.

But all night they heard their makeshift buffers falling. At dawn the work began again.

They lost all count of time. Night followed day with no respite from the merciless assault. What angered the garrison more even than the missiles was the sound of men laughing and singing in the emplacements as they loaded and reloaded their machines. They were having a fine time of it out there: a few hours in the emplacements then back to a good hot meal and a quiet night in their tents. But the garrison were working like flogged animals: eating scraps of bread and cheese, trying to sleep on the hard stone floors with the endless thudding on the walls outside.

All Swayne could do was to work with them, to devise new ways of protecting the walls. In the room over the gatehouse were two sheets of iron that covered the apertures through which they had poured the burning oil on to the mercenaries. He took a party of six men. Dodging the catapult missiles they returned with the sheets to the fortress. They were about five feet square and strongly wrought. Hung down against the fortress wall to cover the most ravaged areas they provided a diversion for the exhausted men, for when a granite missile hit them there was a resounding clang that must have been heard all over the Earl's encampment like a clash of defiance.

Swayne had said that victory lay in the resolution to hold on, but resolution needed physical strength to sustain it, and that was nearly gone. Sleepless nights, the makeshift food, the endless strain of wrenching at buffers that became more shattered every day, the ceaseless concussion of the projectiles, choking dust and bleeding hands: all combined to drag the men towards the limits of endurance.

The time was near when they would no longer be able to keep the walls protected. A few hours of bombardment against the naked stone would bring the fortress down in ruins, and they worked in a daze of exhaustion, merely prolonging a battle already lost.

Towards the end of the second week something happened that the garrison was at first too spent to take in.

All morning the endless assault had ravaged them. It was as if the enemy had sensed their victims to be on the verge of collapse and had redoubled their attack for the final kill. Then suddenly it stopped.

For the first time in what seemed an eternity the 'twang' of the catapults ceased. When the time came round for the next volley from the trebuchets, nothing happened. The silence was unreal. The gulls soared lazily overhead. In the distance a calm sea glittered in the sun. Swayne climbed to the watch tower and looked around him. There was no movement in the emplacements that surrounded them. The shooting arms of the siege engines were poised in the air, but now there was no creaking of winches to draw them back again. It was as if a spell had paralysed the siege.

When he came down from the watch tower the men were beginning to take account of things and pressed him with eager questions.

'What's happened?' they asked. 'What are they doing?'

'Your guess is as good as mine,' said Swayne. 'Maybe they reckon they've knocked us to pieces and are staging an attack to finish us off. If that's their idea they'll get a shock. The ramparts and moat are as sound as ever, so get your bows and take action stations.'

The prospect of letting fly at the besiegers brought life back to the men. It was a joy to get out of the fortress, into the open air, free from the ceaseless pelt of missiles. They lined the ramparts: bows in hands: stacks of arrows beside them: itching to give their tormentors hell.

But nothing happened: no sign of attack: no movement in the enemy encampment. The siege engines in the surrounding emplacements remained silent and inert.

The garrison began to talk of alluring possibilities. Had the Earl run out of money as their commander had predicted? Had his army refused to go on because he couldn't pay them?

Whatever it was, it came as a godsend to the garrison. With no attack in sight they relaxed in the warm sun behind the ramparts. The cooks got busy and brought round canisters of stew: the first hot meal for days.

Swayne couldn't share the wishful hopes of his men. If the Earl had in fact run out of money to pay his men he wouldn't have revealed it in this abrupt, spectacular way. The 'cease fire' had clearly been carried out deliberately to impress or mislead the garrison. Yet if it had been the prelude to a military attack it would surely have come at once, while the garrison was still demoralized by the bombardment. It was possible that a mutiny in the Earl's army had placed another man in command who had ordered the 'cease fire'. Anything was possible. Swayne kept his fingers crossed.

The answer to the mystery came in a way that nobody expected.

A solitary horseman appeared on the hill crest and rode across the fields towards the castle. He was attired magnificently in the Earl's livery: green cloak edged with gold and crimson: plumed helmet gleaming in the sunlight. The big grey horse itself was plumed and covered with a cloth of gold.

There was something preposterous in this splash of pageantry upon a scene so desolate. As the horseman drew nearer Swayne recognized him as the herald who on the first day of the siege had made the ceremonious demand for surrender.

He reined in his horse at the far side of the moat, drew his sword and raised it in ceremonial salute.

'The Earl sends greetings to the garrison,' he called in a loud voice. 'He applauds their valour in holding this castle now beyond defence. In acknowledgement of their courage he grants them their full freedom. He gives word in the King's name that he will permit them to return to their families, and to their peaceful work. In accordance with the law, only the Commander himself must surrender, and that he will do as a man of honour to save his men from the dire penalties of his refusal.

'The Earl gives you an hour to choose between freedom, or death in the final destruction of the castle. If you choose the honourable way for the sake of your families you will lower the drawbridge:

march out in peace and be with them by nightfall.'

With that he saluted and rode away.

Swayne had always known that this might happen. It was a well-used weapon in siege warfare, but it surprised him that it should come when the Earl must have known that he had got the castle at his mercy with no need to offer terms. It suggested to Swayne that things might not be so easy with the Earl as his herald had declared, or that he did not realize how near the fortress was to final collapse.

All this made things no easier for Swayne. With the buffers practically destroyed he knew that a few more hours bombardment would bring the fortress down in ruins. He also knew that the Earl's beguiling promise of freedom for the garrison meant nothing once the Earl had got them in his hands. They and their families would be his slaves when once the castle had surrendered. He could scarcely tell them this without seeming to appeal to them to sacrifice their freedom because he had been offered none himself. Yet to surrender the castle when there was still a remote, fighting chance of pulling through would be a dismal end to a long and valorous defence.

Tom by these problems, his only course was to let the men decide for themselves, with no influence from him, one way or another.

He called his four officers together and said: 'You've heard the Earl's offer to the garrison: there's nothing I can say about this to the men themselves. I must leave them free to make their own decision. I want you to call your groups together and talk to them in your own ways. Put it to them fair and square. Don't try to force them one way or the other. I shall go to my room, and when you are ready, come and give me their decision.'

Chapter Nine

If the truce called for a hard decision from the garrison, it was no less a racking hour of suspense for Conrad.

'In five days,' he had assured the Earl, 'we shall have launched such a hurricane of missiles that the fortress will be destroyed. The survivors, with no shelter left for them, will welcome surrender with open arms.'

Things hadn't gone quite as Conrad had predicted. When he had seen the garrison padding the walls with old cowhides he had laughed it off as futile. His missiles would soon pulverize them, and as the granite balls scoured deeper, the fortress would begin to fall in massive fragments and the garrison, driven into the open, would be slaughtered by the projectiles from the mangonels. Conrad had been delighted by the power and accuracy of his machines, but at the end of the predicted five days, despite the storm of missiles the fortress still stood there in its bruised and mangled padding.

The Earl had kept asking the maddening question, 'The fortress? Why aren't you destroying the fortress? You said five days?'

Conrad had been reassuring. The padding of the walls had delayed them a little, he said, but it was not a real protection. The tremendous impact of those granite missiles was steadily loosening and cracking the foundations. When finally the foundations crumbled the fortress would collapse.

Every night the Earl had lain sleepless in his bed, listening to the concussion of the projectors against the crossbeams of the trebuchets, hoping each time to hear a crashing fall of masonry. But every morning, when he looked out from his pavilion, the fortress still stood there, apparently unscathed.

Conrad had barely slept at all. Day and night he moved tirelessly from one emplacement to another: testing the machines: occasionally ordering small adjustments and repairs. He could see that the garrison were hanging all manner of incongruous, makeshift protectors against the walls and hoped that it signalled the end of their resources. Yet somehow, and some way they carried on.

The day came when Conrad was forced into a crisis. He told the Earl that the destruction of the fortress was not the vital issue. The mangonels had thrown thousands of missiles into the castle that would kill or maim. The granite balls, crashing against the fortress wall, would have reduced the survivors to physical and mental wrecks. The time had come to end their sufferings with a merciful surrender.

And so at the end of ten days of blitzkrieg he had advised the Earl to send his herald forward.

Conrad had rehearsed the herald in what he was to say. The garrison, he knew, were local men with families in the surrounding farms and villages. An offer of freedom to return safely to them that night, with a thinly veiled threat that their wives and children would suffer for it otherwise: what man could possibly shout defiance?

Towards the end of the truce Conrad laid on another threat to help the garrison decide. He ordered every siege weapon to reload, making as much display of it as possible.

There was another more impelling reason why Conrad desperately prayed for the garrison to submit: something he dared not tell the Earl. He strolled to and fro beside the pavilion with a debonair display of confidence. 'If they don't surrender,' he said to the Earl, 'they'll be signing their own death warrants. Another day, and we'll smash what's left of them to pieces.' But all the time his anxious eyes were upon the drawbridge of the castle: praying to see it lowered as a signal of surrender.

Swayne sat waiting in his room at the top of the war-scarred fortress.

What were his leaders saying to the men? What would their decision be?

Sometimes he was near hoping that they would decide upon surrender. They had fought so valiantly that they deserved to live and return to their families. He knew that it would amount to little more than slavery. The Earl would make his conquest sure by turning them out of their farms and putting his own people in. It was fine to cry defiance and declare it better to be dead than slaves, but heroics aside it was better to be slaves caring for their families than dead men leaving wives and children helpless and alone.

For himself, he knew that the Earl would waste no time in hanging him. His one bitter regret was that he had not sent Roger to the safety of the Monastery. But Roger was now doomed as surely as he himself.

For the castle it mattered little now. Another day of merciless bombardment and the fortress was bound to fall. Better for the men to surrender than prolong the agony to the end.

The waiting dragged on. Swayne was too tired to think clearly any longer. In any case there were no more decisions for him to make: no more orders to be given. He could only wait for the final verdict of his men.

At last he heard his leaders climbing the turret steps: slow dragging footsteps, it seemed, of men who came with a desolate message. Swayne heard them stop at the head of the steps and mutter together in low voices. Were they deciding who should break the fatal news?

He heard them coming along the passage, their boots crunching through mortar and fragments of stone shaken down by the bombardment. Bernard was the senior of them: a brawny farmer whom the young men called 'the bull'. He had played his part so well throughout the siege that Swayne had made him second in command. If the men had yoted for surrender, Swayne trusted him now to do his best for them, and for all the people in the settlement.

They came into the room. Bernard had never been a man for words. He preferred to do things rather than to talk. He hesitated, cleared his throat. 'We talked to the men . . .' he started, and dried up.

'We'll?' said Swayne. 'And what was their reply?'

Bernard began again, this time more deliberately.

'We talked to the men,' he repeated, 'in the way you told us to. We put it to them fair and square, not trying to persuade them one way or another. And to a man they said they'd see the Earl in hell before they gave in to him.'

Bernard stopped abruptly. It was a long speech for him to make, longer than any that Swayne had ever heard from him.

Maybe it was because he was so physically tired, so mentally exhausted that Swayne found it hard to keep himself from the indignity of breaking down before his leaders.

'Are you telling me, honestly, that this was the free decision of them all?'

One of the others answered.

'We talked to our groups separately,' he said, 'none of us knowing what the others were doing. And we only met together when we had finished. There wasn't a man who even spoke a word about surrender.'

'One of my fellows,' put in another, 'said that if their Commander voted for surrender they'd lock him up and carry on without him.'

With that all four broke into a great laugh of release.

There was one thing, said Bernard, that the men had specially asked permission for.

There were four small catapult machines upon the ramparts. Several times, during the bombardment, the garrison had wanted to use them in reprisal but Swayne had forbidden it. Small missiles would have been useless against the impregnable emplacements of the enemy.

But now they had begged for the joy and satisfaction of letting loose a few to show their defiance, and Swayne could deny them nothing.

'Let them shoot to their heart's content,' he said. 'But tell them to keep their heads down.'

It was almost upon deadline of the truce when the garrison let fly with their catapults at the enemy emplacements. They were simple machines that threw a missile no larger than a cricket ball but with every shot they let out a cheer of exultation. It was a joy to release the pent up frustration of those endless days of impotence. Every missile hit the emplacement walls with a heart-lifting thud. They did no damage, but it was a fine gesture of defiance.

Swayne gave them time to let off steam then ordered them back to the shelter of the fortress. He knew what they must now expect, and it wasn't long in coming. At the blast of a horn from the Earl's headquarters every siege engine around the castle let fly. It was as if the besiegers were maddened by the garrison's defiance. Missiles from the mangonels came raining down; two massive granite balls from the trebuchets crashed against the fortress within seconds of each other.

Stripped almost bare of its protection the fortress shuddered from the blows. Broken stone came showering down: loosened stones inside the fortress were falling with each impact.

The Earl's hope of softening the garrison with enticing promises had backfired on him. It had put iron into the men. They set to with redoubled vigour to replace the remaining buffers that still gave some protection. They hunted the fortress for the last things that would serve. They strung together the wooden stools from the hall and tied up bundles of spare clothing.

For Swayne there was something pitiful in that final gesture of defiance. He knew that they had rejected surrender through a blind, instinctive trust that in some way, somehow, he would see them through to victory. He had nothing to give them now. He could only work with them, encouraging them, putting up a show of hope and make-believe when he knew in his heart that the reopening of that merciless bombardment could only spell the end.

All night the assault went on.

With most of the protection gone the balls were striking the naked walls like crashes of thunder. Swayne walked around the rooms and passages, watching for fissures in the walls that would mark the end. He watched as the captain of an old ship might watch the bulwarks of his vessel battered by a raging storm.

At dawn they had just begun a hopeless attempt to replace a few surviving bolsters when one of the granite missiles made further efforts useless. It crashed straight into a deep cavity already made. Until then the shots had sent a shower of broken stone down the outer wall: this time the sound of tumbling masonry came from inside the fortress.

Swayne went up the turret steps and found a gaping hole in the wall of the main hall: the granite missile lying among the debris on the floor. It was the first to make a clean break through. It had struck near the raftered ceiling, and a heavy oak beam, stripped almost bare of its support, rested precariously on a solitary baulk of stone.

It was enough to tell Swayne that the fortress was now a death trap. A direct blow on that sole surviving support could bring the rafter down and with it the whole upper structure of the building.

'Get the men outside,' he told his officers. 'Let them take cover against the sheltered walls.'

It was the order of a captain to desert a sinking ship.

There was a measure of safety, crouched up against the side walls of the fortress untouched by the granite missiles, but for Swayne it was a move of desperation. If the fortress fell in ruins he would have saved his men, but with nothing to sustain them. Their food supplies, their vital source of drinking water, everything would be buried under a massive pile of wreckage.

He had to give them some sort of hope.

'If a shot brings down those oak supporting beams,' he told them, 'the inside of the building will give way. If we hear a crashing and a tumbling inside, we must run for it and take protection behind the ramparts. Even if we lose the fortress, there's still a way to carry on the fight. After dark we'll cross the moat and make a break-through between the emplacements: make our way to one of the fishing villages and build up new defences with our backs to the sea and plenty of extra men to fight with us.'

It was a chance in a hundred, if Swayne could give it even that, but it put new heart into the men. To fight with the sea at their backs appealed to them. Two men risked the peril of the fortress to go in and get a bucket of water from the well and a few oat cakes from the kitchen. They drank and passed the food around.

For hours they crouched there. Some slept from exhaustion: others cracked jokes. Father Peter began a song and the men joined in the chorus.

And all the while the granite balls came whistling over to crash against the walls. Swayne held his breath at every impact: prepared for the ominous thudding of falling beams that would spell the end of the old fortress that had met the assault so well.

Yet by what seemed a miracle it still survived.

It was towards evening when the siege engines began to behave in a strange, unfathomable way.

The first sign came when a shot from a trebuchet soared over the fortress without touching it.

For two weeks the missiles had been striking with such unerring accuracy that Swayne's first reaction to this unexpected 'sky shot' was that the enemy had some special purpose in it. Maybe a signal for some new development. What followed was even stranger and more inexplicable. The next shots hit the fortress but without their usual force. They came over in a tired, half-hearted way and dropped to the ground without scarring the walls. They were followed by some shots that went grotesquely wide.

For a time the small mangonel machines went on shooting their missiles, then they too began to lose direction. Some fell short of the castle ramparts, sending up splashes of water from the moat or bounding harmlessly in the field outside.

The big trebuchets were silent for a while. Then they opened up again with results even worse than before. The big granite balls went all over the place: some soaring right over the fortress and landing among their own emplacements on the other side.

And then there were no more. The siege engines all round the castle seemed tired out.

Swayne was completely baffled. If the whole thing was an elaborate trick then they had played it to absurdity. They must have seen that the padding on the fortress walls was totally destroyed: that their missiles were striking the naked stone. They would have known that the fortress was at last at their mercy.

Whatever had happened, it gave the garrison a heavensent respite.

The sun had set. It was growing twilight. The Earl wouldn't hazard an attack on the ramparts by night. If an attack was brewing it would come at dawn. The men above all things needed rest. With the fortress in its precarious condition Swayne told the garrison to find places to sleep in the outbuildings around the ramparts.

He posted a few sentries around the walls, and spent the night with them on watch, still puzzling over the strange way of things, and what would happen in the dawn.

If Swayne had been mystified that evening. there was no mystery in it for the unhappy Conrad.

He had known from the start that the strain upon his siege engines would put a term upon their effective life, but they had ample power to demolish the fortress long before that happened. When the garrison padded the fortress walls it seemed to him a fleabite to siege engines with such massive power. But in all his experiments he had concentrated upon the one purpose of knocking down a wall of stone. It had never occurred to him to experiment against a bolster stuffed with straw. Silly things like that weren't worth a thought.

He wasn't greatly worried by the persistence of the garrison in replacing the shattered bolsters. They would all be soon destroyed, and the ceaseless bombardment from the catapults must make their work insufferable. But when a week had passed, with the fortress still surviving, he began to notice ominous signs of wear in the siege engines: the ropes and cables were beginning to fray, the cogs in the winding gear were slipping, small fissures were beginning to show in the crossbeams that took the impact of the shooting arms, the shafts of the mangonels were losing their resilience.

It was then that he advised the Earl to call a truce and demand surrender, without telling him the desperate need for it. There was, he believed, a good chance that the bluff would succeed.

When after that nerve-racking truce the garrison had shot those puny little missiles in defiance it was a challenge for a final, desperate gamble. All night he went tirelessly from emplacement to emplacement, watching the teams at work, praying that the machines would hold. In the morning his hopes bounded when he saw that a missile had penetrated the fortress wall at a vital point between the supporting beams. He could see a beam projecting from the cavity. perilously held by a narrow pillar of stone. He saw too that the garrison were no longer working on the summit of the fortress attempting to replace the buffers. They had clearly deserted it. A dozen more shots would bring those massive beams crashing down with the whole fortress with them.

It was maddening, with success in his grasp, to realize that his siege engines were slowly losing power. One shot alone, at the vital point, was all now needed, but the granite balls had lost their accuracy, striking the walls away from the vital area. With every volley he held his breath. praying that one lucky shot would find its mark.

But in that last assault he had driven his siege engines beyond the limit of their endurance. In one of the big trebuchets the crossbeam had loosened in its bedding of cement, in the other the cables had given way. Emergency repairs were impossible. The small catapult machines had long been wearing out. The constant strain had robbed them of their spring. They were now behaving so erratically that most of the missiles never reached the castle, but with the collapse of the big trebuchets the catapults counted for little. Conrad sent the word around for a cease fire.

He was now in a dismal plight. The Earl had put a small fortune into those siege engines upon assurance of quick victory. What was he to tell him now?

The failure went far beyond an explanation to the Earl. It threatened his whole future as an engineer of siege weapons superior to any yet conceived. On the Continent that summer he had produced an engine with spectacular results. A few shots at a castle had wrought such unexpected damage that a stubborn garrison had immediately surrendered. His name was made. It got around that here was a man who could crush castle walls like egg shells.

He had taken the job at Swayne Castle as a 'guinea pig' for his experiments, expecting it to be a walkover. He hadn't known how different it would be from one of those chivalrous continental affairs when a castle owner, seeing his property being badly damaged, would make a ceremonial surrender and invite his opponent to dine with him. He had discovered that amateur soldiers fighting for their homes and families were more than a match against a professional fighting for prestige and money.

He had got to cook up an explanation for the Earl and went to see his friend Raymond about it. Raymond gave him little sympathy or consolation, but his own prestige was bound up with the failure, and the two men put their heads together. They worked out an answer and went to see the Earl.

The Earl was looking tired and ill, but fuming with impatience.

'Why have you stopped the bombardment?' he demanded. 'Why are you giving them this opportunity to rest, and repair the damage?'

'The siege engines have broken down,' said Conrad. 'For that we must blame the Royal Armoury at Norwich for supplying us with faulty equipment. The ropes and cables had been in store too long and quickly lost their strength and pliancy. The iron framework was weak. The winches were made of wood that had not matured and the cogs have given way.'

This wasn't good enough for the Earl.

'But heavens above!' he shouted. 'As an expert you surely must have noticed this when it was offered to you! Why didn't you refuse the stuff?'

'These things only show themselves when put to the test,' replied Conrad. 'Had they stood the strain for a few more hours they would have completed the ruin of the fortress.'

'How long will it take you to repair them?' asked the Earl.

This was a question that Conrad had hoped to avoid. He well knew that it wasn't faulty material, but those accursed bolsters that had beaten him. If he spent a month rebuilding his machines the garrison would have ample time to repair the damage and make new and better bolsters. He began to explain how difficult it would be to replace the vital components. The Royal Armoury having let them down and with the country in the grip of civil war it would be very difficult indeed . . .

He started to explain the highly technical requirements but the Earl had had enough of it.

'The less I hear about these futile machines the better!' he shot out. 'They've been a miserable and expensive failure, and you must now get back to what I wanted from the start. You have already told me that the bombardment must have killed or maimed the greater part of the garrison. You'll have no difficulty at all in taking the castle now by direct assault, and that you must do without delay.'

Raymond and Conrad were expecting this, and had good reasons for avoiding it. They knew for a fact that the bombardment hadn't 'killed or maimed' the garrison. They had seen the number of sound and vigorous men who had lined the ramparts to shoot off their catapults at the end of the truce. The moat and the ramparts remained unscathed. An open assault would be as difficult as ever.

And Raymond had another worry on his hands. His mercenaries expected their commander to lead them to a swift and overwhelming victory. This had always happened in the past. They had looked up to Raymond as a man who never failed, but now they had suffered two humiliating defeats: first at the gatehouse and now with the bombardment Raymond knew that their trust in him was badly shaken. If he drove them now into the desperate hazards of a direct assault he would probably have a mutiny on his hands, and he wasn't going to risk it.

He therefore put forward a plan that in the circumstances was obviously the best.

'There is one weapon,' he said, 'that has never failed: the weapon of starvation. We have kept these men imprisoned in their castle for three months. Their food reserves can never have been large. By now they are bound to be on short rations: every day will make it harder for them. Why sacrifice good fighting men when with a little time and patience the castle and its surviving garrison will fall into your hands without a blow?'

The Earl didn't like it. His martial ardour called for a military victory. There was something sordid and undignified in sitting down and waiting for the garrison to starve. It was practically a confession of defeat, and yet there was something comforting about it: no more anxieties; no more risks of humiliating military disaster. And something very satisfactory about sitting down to dinner at night in his pavilion thinking of those hated Swaynes starving to death behind their castle walls. As for his son, Gregory, the Earl couldn't care less what happened to him.

'Very well,' he said, 'we will starve them out. It certainly won't take long. But if in the meantime an opportunity comes to capture the castle by assault, I depend upon you to do so without a day's delay.'

And to that the two young mercenary Captains readily agreed.

Chapter Ten

The garrison had their best sleep for many a night and when they woke up to find themselves sprawled around in the outbuildings it took some time to sort out what had happened. The sun had been up for hours but when no attack developed at dawn Swayne had left them undisturbed.

The emplacements around the castle were deserted. The shooting arms of the siege engines stuck out above the bulwarks at crazy lopsided angles like the masts of sunken ships. The only sign of life were the long-familiar sentries, slowly patrolling between the guard tents.

The cooks went into the fortress and got some food. They made a fire in the open: prepared some breakfast, and when the men had eaten Swayne talked to them.

'Why they laid off the bombardment I don't know,' he said. 'I expected an attack overland but it hasn't come. All that matters now is to clear things up and be ready for whatever the Earl has got up his sleeve. The first job is the fortress. It's taken a hard beating and we'll see what we can do about it.'

With the masons he examined the structure from foundations to the summit. The foundations were deep down in the solid chalk and the masons found no cracks in the vaults or dungeon. The trouble began about midway up its height where the enemy had concentrated the assault. The two sides exposed to the bombardment were a sorry sight, pitted with holes that in some places overlapped to make wide, jagged wounds. None had penetrated right through except the missile that had almost dislodged an oak beam. The masons judged that if they could make this beam secure the fortress would be safe for occupation.

A working party mixed cement and the masons began the hazardous business of strutting the precarious beam. They used the best of the stones shot down to rebuild the wall around the beam. Elsewhere in the building they cemented back the loose stones shaken out by the concussions.

The men had never been in higher spirits. It was a joy to work out in the open after days shut in the twilit fortress, free from the endless catapult missiles and the dust and destruction of the granite balls.

The carpenters repaired the broken stools and table tops that were hung out in the last emergency. The bed mattresses battered by the missiles were restuffed and stitched together: the tapestries from the hall, with honourable scars and holes in them, were hung on the walls again and bed clothes that had been stuffed with straw were unrolled and hung up to air. The dust and debris were swept from the rooms and passages and the fortress was fit to live in again. The cooks stoked the fire outside and prepared a bounteous midday meal.

The men had been too busy on repair work to give much thought to the enemy, but sitting out there at their meal in the sunlight they began to make guesses about his strange behaviour, and what it was all about. Most of the men reckoned that the Earl had shot his bolt. He had failed to break in at the gatehouse and failed with his bombardment. What else could he now do? The answer was to pack up and go. He had given priceless time to repair the damaged fortress. If he tried an assault overland the garrison would be delighted. They were hardened soldiers now. If he made an attempt to bridge the moat and scale the ramparts they would give him hell.

They relaxed and stretched out with nothing to disturb them until a man keeping watch on the ramparts called out, 'Here's that man coming on his horse again!'

They crowded on to the ramparts to watch the herald in all his finery riding in flamboyant dignity towards them. He looked more incongruous than ever, threading his way between the deserted emplacements: the symbol of failure and defeat, but he had all the old assurance as he rode up to the moat and raised his sword in salutation.

'The Earl sends greetings,' he announced, 'but deplores your foolish rejection of the freedom offered you to return to your families without punishment.

'He leaves the offer open for another hour but if you persist beyond that time he will hold you prisoners in this castle until you starve.

'You are surrounded and cannot escape. The Earl will continue this siege for months if need be, and when starvation finally forces you to surrender you will not be free, as you are today, to return to your families in peace and with honour, but will be hanged from the ramparts of this castle as traitors to the King.'

The men gave him a derisive cheer as he rode away, but it was something they hadn't expected. When they saw him coming they imagined that the Earl was sending some sort of proposal for peace. A face-saving expedient to cover up his failure. Starvation, they reckoned, was a threat that the Earl had pulled out of his hat for the want of anything better; a puny threat compared with his formidable assaults.

Swayne brushed aside the Earl's new offer of surrender. It was, he told his men, a plain confession of military defeat. The Earl had failed to take the castle by force and given it up as hopeless. 'But if he thinks he can sit down and wait for us to starve there are certain things he hasn't made allowance for.'

'The summer's nearly over,' Swayne said. 'So far the Earl's army has had the best of it, sitting out there in the sunlight with us shut in the fortress. But what's it going to be like out there in those flimsy tents when the autumn gales come roaring in and it pours with rain? – And the roads that bring his stores up are deep in mud? The Earl never reckoned on being here beyond the summer. How's he going to feel when an icy storm blows his trashy pavilion down: and he has to go on forking out sacks of money to pay his army? I'd sooner be here in this old fortress with log fires blazing, and this is where we'll be until the Earl has had enough of it out there in the mud and rain.'

There were certain things he didn't tell them. There wasn't any point in burdening them with problems that they couldn't answer. He reserved those problems for his officers in private.

'So go ahead and get the fortress ready for dinner in the hall tonight, and I think you can take it for granted that we shall dine in peace.'

Later that day Swayne called his officers together to talk about the things he didn't want the men to know. The castle had been well provisioned but Swayne had staked a great deal on the livestock. Grazing on good pasture the cows and goats would provide the milk for cheese and butter well into the winter. With eggs from the poultry and fish from the moat they would draw very lightly on food from store, and Father Peter had predicted that with care they could last out beyond Christmas; far beyond the Earl's capacity to continue the siege. That was what the garrison had understood, and why they didn't worry about the Earl's starvation threat.

But the worst effect of the bombardment hadn't been the damage to the fortress. On several nights there had been heavy rain. The grassland had been waterlogged and the countless missiles from the catapults had churned it into a quagmire. It was more like ploughed land than a pasture field: useless for cattle to graze on. They would have to be slaughtered before they got too thin to use as food. That went for the poultry too, and the supply of fresh food would be over.

It meant new calculations for Father Peter, in charge of rations. 'I can't say exactly until I've worked things out,' he said, 'but when we are dependent entirely upon our food in store I'd say that about six weeks will see the end of it.'

There was something else that worried Swayne. He had often told the men of the huge expense of the Earl's army: that with all his money he couldn't keep it up for long. But if he had now settled for a starvation siege he could send the majority of his army home. The mercenaries alone would be sufficient to keep the stranglehold, with a couple of hundred levies to man the guard posts. When the herald had said that the Earl could sustain the siege 'for months if need be' he was no doubt telling the plain truth.

Father Peter said that strict rationing imposed at once would stretch their food supplies for an extra few weeks, but what was the point? – If the Earl, as now seemed certain, could keep up the siege, indefinitely, what difference would it make to eke out their reserves to last eight weeks instead of six?

When military assault had been the main concern Swayne kept his men informed from day to day, strengthening their resolution with a good measure of hope. But starvation couldn't be defeated by resolution. Hope couldn't be manufactured from thin air.

'Say nothing to the men about all this,' he told his officers. 'There's nothing to gain and a lot to lose by telling them how we stand when there isn't a thing they can do about it. I'd sooner they had good rations for six weeks than keep them half starved for eight. They've done a fine job and deserve a reward so we'll give them a good feed in the hall tonight.'

A log fire was set roaring in the wide hearth of the hall. The previous 'celebration' had been laid on by Swayne as a desperate measure when the men had been near breaking point. The granite missiles had been crashing against the walls, and the men had nothing to look forward to but a night of misery.

This time it was different. Beyond the ramparts lay the derelict, defeated siege weapons. In the morning there would be no straining to replace the worn-out buffers: no danger from the catapults. They could sleep in peace and in the morning could set up their targets for practice with their bows and walk freely on the ramparts.

Swayne had told the cook to put a dozen chickens in the stewpot. They would have to go anyway, now that there was no meadowland to feed them and no grain to spare. Father Peter salvaged some mutilated cabbages from his bombarded vegetable garden and brought in a sack of watercress from the moat side. There was wine, and fresh-baked bread, and jars of fruit preserved in honey.

On the previous night the hall was derelict: a shambles of debris and fallen stone. Now the lamps were lit, the tapestries hung around the walls. When the meal was over they gathered around the fire. The musicians got out their instruments and the men sang in chorus.

It was a happy carefree evening and Swayne and his officers

closed their eyes to the future and enjoyed the 'victory supper' with their men.

One of Swayne's problems during the bombardment was what to do with Gregory.

When the Earl let fly with his missiles Gregory had offered to help in the defence, but it wasn't in keeping with the rules of war for an enemy prisoner to assist against his own side, especially when the assaulting commander happened to be his own father. Swayne had accordingly told him to keep to his room.

Gregory had resented this for reasons that he could never have made Swayne understand, or in fact explain logically to himself.

He was in fact a neutral in this war. He couldn't accept his father's reasons for beginning it and considered that the Swaynes were sensible to fight back. But having got mixed up in it he enjoyed it as an adventure that had never come his way before. When he had offered to help the Swaynes to defend their castle he wasn't deliberately siding against his father. He merely wanted to make some return for the hospitality that the Swaynes had given him.

He returned to the status of a prisoner, except that his door remained unlocked.

It was then that Roger discovered Gregory's complete detachment from the war. During an exhausting, nerve-racking day Roger would go to his room and find Gregory standing in the window alcove, watching the siege engines at work. They were on the topmost floor of the fortress. The missiles were concentrated upon the wall beneath but some were striking very close to them. Gregory was quite impervious to the danger. He seemed in fact to enjoy it. He would scarcely move when a missile struck nearby and made the fortress quiver. He would brush off the dust that fell from the ceiling and say, 'That was a good shot,' then laugh and say to Roger, 'They won't knock this old fortress down if they try for a hundred years!'

He only showed annoyance once. When they were trying to get some sleep, and a near one crashed against the wall outside, he turned over with a growl and said, 'Why doesn't the old fool shut up and go to bed?'

When the truce was declared, and the herald gave the garrison an hour to choose between surrender or destruction, Swayne had seen little chance for any of them to survive and gave Gregory his freedom to leave the castle and go back to his father.

'If you do that,' said Gregory, 'he'll take it that you've given up and are using me to soften him. If I stay here he'll know he hasn't beaten you, and he's a long way from doing that.'

He wasn't trying to be heroic. He just wanted to see fair play on both sides.

So Gregory had stayed, and Roger was glad, for Gregory, with his humour and contempt for danger, had been a tonic for him in the darkest hours.

For a few days the garrison basked in their new-found freedom. They got back to the recreations and exercises that kept them fit. Above all they enjoyed the freedom of the open air. Swayne kept up the routine of guard duties to keep his men employed rather than from any need. Apart from the sentries patrolling between the guard tents the enemy ignored the castle as if it didn't exist. They had now settled down to wait for the inmates to starve.

Swayne and his officers kept up the pretence that all was well: that they had only to wait for the winter rains and gales to force the Earl to give up and go home. But they knew that bar a miracle their food supplies would be gone far sooner than the Earl.

The novelty of an easy life wore off and the men got bored and restless. They had been under siege for three months. What got them down was the placid inactivity of the enemy. Guard duties had once a flavour of adventure, always on the alert for new movements by the besiegers. It meant nothing now but boredom.

For a time they kept the cows alive by ferrying men across the moat at night to stuff sacks with grass from beyond the ramparts. But cows needed to roam fields and chew fresh pasture. They grew thin, stopped giving milk, and had to be slaughtered.

The slaughter of the livestock brought home to the garrison that things were not so easy as their officers made out. The poultry, starved of food, had already gone into the stewpot. A cow, thin and tough, could barely sustain forty men for a week. With no eggs or milk they were down to the unappetizing stuff in store.

One day Roger got an idea.

He went to his father's room and said: 'You remember the night when I got through the sentry lines and went through the woods to the sea? – The woods were teeming with rabbits, racing about in all directions, bolting down their burrows. If we get through and set snares we could go back each night and collect enough for dinner.'

It wasn't a new idea. Swayne and his officers had often talked of the possibilities of foraging for food, but the nearest supply was far away: in the farms and coastal villages. The amount needed for a garrison of forty men could scarcely be smuggled between the guard tents. The idea of collecting a few rabbits in the woods had been considered and discarded. The risks didn't measure up to such a trivial return.

But Roger was so insistent that his father began to listen.

'Those men at the guard tents are a sleepy lot,' he said, 'They're not the mercenaries. They're only the levies. If I could get through in the days when they were new to it and on the alert I'm sure we could do it now if we went about it carefully. Half a dozen of us in single file, crawling through the long grass could get through at night and come back with a dozen rabbits – a better dinner than hard salt pork!'

Swayne hesitated. It had always been his first concern to keep the garrison up to strength against any assault the Earl might stage. He would never have risked the loss of any of them in a foray that was inessential. But what did it matter now, when the Earl was unlikely to attack, and their own supplies were draining out?

There was another reason in favour of what Roger had suggested. The men were sinking into a state of lethargy. They were dispirited, disillusioned. They needed something to raise their hopes and this might be the answer.

When he told the garrison it put new life into them. It offered everything they wanted: release from boredom, a spice of adventure, the chance of knocking a hole in the Earl's starvation scheme; and above all the promise of some rabbit stew. He had to damp down their enthusiasm with a warning of the dangers. A moment of carelessness, a faulty move, a cough or a sneeze, and the whole thing would be over, not merely for that night but for good and all.

'These sentries may be bored and off their guard,' he said, 'but the slightest sound, a shadow against the skyline, a track left in the grass and they'll be on the alert, waiting for you the next night – probably with doubled sentries.'

They spent the next day watching the enemy guard posts. They were familiar with the daily routine but now studied it more closely.

The guard tents were manned by two shifts: one for the day and one for the night. Five men were posted at each guard tent.

In the afternoon a wagon arrived with supplies, leaving at each guard tent logs for the fires and food for the men. An officer rode round for a casual inspection. Towards sunset the night shift came on. They knew that the Earl's levies were on duty all day. If the mercenaries took over during the night it would be a tougher proposition. But at sunset they were glad to see a company of levies arriving to take over. The mercenaries apparently disdained the humdrum job of sentry duty, remaining in their camp on call for emergency.

When the night shift arrived they made up their fires to cook their evening meal, and well into the night the garrison could see the glowing fires. This too was in favour of Swayne's men. Sitting around bright fires the eyes of the sentries would be less attuned to the darkness around them.

Roger had claimed the right to guide the first foraging party because he had got through the sentry lines before. His job on that observation day was to choose the best point for the intrusion. There were undulations in the ground that separated the guard tents and Roger settled upon a gap with a slight declivity where the shadows would be heavier, with less chance of a crawling man being seen against the skyline.

Next day they spent preparing. Swayne chose half a dozen of the youngest, lightest men who could move most easily and leave no tracks in the grass. They carried no weapons to impede them or rattle as they moved. They blacked their hands and faces and carried snaring nets around their waists.

It was a fine, dark, moonless night. They ferried across the moat and went stealthily forward through the long meadow grass.

They passed one of the big trebuchet emplacements on their way, ghostly and sinister, with its shooting arm projecting above the bulwarks, untouched since it had sent its last failing missile at the fortress. Roger was glad when they were by it. There was something so menacing about it that he imagined mercenaries still lurking there in wait for them.

The guard tents lay a hundred yards ahead: each clearly marked by the fire beside it. They got down on their knees and crawled towards the gap that Roger had chosen for the breakthrough. When they judged that they were close to the track of the patrolling sentries they lay still and waited for a man to pass and slip through when he had gone.

Things didn't happen as they had expected. Lurking there in the darkness they could see the guard tents on either side with men sitting round the brazier fires, cooking meat on skewers. They were talking and laughing, more interested in their food than in keeping watch. It was soon clear that they had given up the patrol by night: at least with any regularity. They patrolled by day to show the castle that it was surrounded, but there wasn't much point in wandering to and fro by night. The camp fires were sufficient to show they were on guard. They had clearly not been briefed to look out for a few men crawling through the grass to catch some rabbits.

When assured that the way was clear Roger crawled forward with the men beside him. They were soon across the sentry track and making for the dark woods ahead. It was a joy to be in those friendly woods that they had known so well in days gone by. They had planned to net some burrows and collect the results next night, but when they saw rabbits bolting down their holes they spread nets across and stamped around the surrounding ground. The startled rabbits came racing out into the nets and in half an hour they had a dozen. Each man tied a couple around his waist and they began their homeward journey.

By now the sentries at the guard tents had cooked their food and were sitting around the braziers enjoying it. One was strumming on a guitar: some were singing. Swayne's men crawled stealthily back the way they had come, and were soon back in the castle. The foragers were greeted by the garrison with jubilation. They had punched a hole in the Earl's own net and got a bounteous rabbit stew.

Roger couldn't contain his pride at the success. 'I don't think those sentries would have cared if they'd seen us,' he told his father. 'After all, they aren't really enemies. They're only here because the Earl made them come. They've nothing against us and we've nothing against them. If we'd run straight into them and told them we were only after rabbits I reckon they'd have said good luck and go ahead.'

Roger needed damping down.

'They may not be our enemies,' said Swayne: 'they might even like to make friends, but it would be at the risk of their lives, and they know it. If the Earl discovered they were letting you through he'd have them flogged and hanged for it. So for heaven's sake be careful and treat them as your deadly enemies.'

From the summit of the fortress they kept watch next day upon the land between the guard tents where the foragers had crossed. If tracks in the grass had been discovered, or any sort of evidence had been left behind there would be inspections and a hunt around for clues. But nothing happened. The sentries continued their lazy patrols, quite unconcerned. An officer rode around as usual without showing any special interest. It was clear that the first foray had left no evidence behind.

For the second foray the whole garrison wanted to be included, but Swayne kept the team to the same six men, adding two more to be initiated. And he gave them a forceful lecture on the need for care, stressing that the smallest lapse in vigilance would spell the end of it.

Roger led the party on a different route to avoid making a beaten track. The same routine at the guard tents was going on: men cooking their supper over the braziers, laughing and talking. The party slipped through as before and were soon in the safety of the woods. The nets laid the previous night had plenty of struggling rabbits in them, but they moved the nets to burrows deeper in the woods, out of range of casual excursions by the enemy.

The nightly foraging became a regular routine. They went out while the enemy sentries were cooking their supper and came back while they were eating it. One night they were alarmed to see a man wandering towards them and they lay immobile in the long grass, but he had only come to obey the call of nature and soon returned to the warmth and comfort of his camp fire.

The Earl and his army were apparently satisfied that the garrison was pent up starving in the castle, with no hope of escape. The sentries at the guard tents were merely there to remind the garrison that they were surrounded, and that was all there was to it. After their supper one man remained on duty sitting beside the fire. The other went into their tents to sleep.

Swayne's men gained experience but never relaxed their vigilance. They varied their points of incursion and when sufficient men were trained Swayne sent out two nightly parties from opposite sides of the castle.

Nobody was more thankful than Father Peter to see fresh food arriving every night. With a breakfast of fish from the moat and an ample dinner of rabbit stew he was only drawing grain from store. There was wild fruit in the woods at that time of the year. He made the men take satchels to stuff with nuts and berries; small apples, hips and haws and quincies. He had the fruit stewed down for syrup to go with the oat cakes. Some nights they caught partridges and pheasants and took care to drop no feathers on the journey back.

The time had now passed when the Earl could have reasonably expected the castle to be starved out. He would be watching daily for some token of surrender, and when it didn't come he would naturally suspect that the garrison was smuggling in provisions from outside. He would take steps to plug the loopholes, probably double the guard and lay on patrols.

To avoid this danger Swayne called for a volunteer to pose as a deserter.

They staged the affair with spectacular trimmings.

One morning the man swam the moat and ran towards the enemy guard tents. Some of the garrison stood on the ramparts and put up a great show of anger. They shouted abuse at him: yelled at him to come back and fired some arrows safely wide. Reaching the enemy lines, dirty and dishevelled, he pleaded for mercy and begged desperately for food.

He was taken before the Earl and told a pitiful story. The garrison, he said, was starving, seething with mutiny, yearning to surrender, but the Commander was forcing them to hold on and to die together. For himself, the man said, he could bear it no longer. He had a wife and children in one of the outlying farms and had summoned up his remaining strength to escape. He begged the Earl to give him pardon and allow him to return to his family.

The Earl was very gratified. It was the news that he had been waiting for. It pleased him so much that he ordered the man to be given food and allowed to depart and rejoin his family. The man stammered his gratitude and set off along the inland road. When out of sight of the enemy he slipped into the woods and returned to wait and join up with the foraging party that evening.

Swayne had another reason for deceiving the Earl. He hoped that the gruesome account of their desperate plight would draw the Earl into a final assault to get the thing over and done with. He was sure that his men, in their present high spirits, could give the Earl's army a resounding beating if it tried to bridge the moat and the shock would persuade the Earl to take his demoralized army home before the winter storms played havoc with their camp.

On that score Swayne was disappointed. The enemy made no move. It seemed that the Earl had decided to sit things out. It didn't trouble Swayne overmuch. In view of the 'deserter's' story the Earl wasn't likely to increase his guard around the castle, and the foraging expeditions were going so well that it gave them some new, more adventurous ideas.

Why not send messengers to the nearest farm and fishing village? – Arrange for supplies of fresh meat and sea food to be brought up at night to the woods for the garrison to collect on their foraging expeditions?

There was an even more alluring project. If they could smuggle food they could smuggle men. New men could be brought in to replace the garrison who could go on a week's leave to their homes.

Swayne saw no problem. Confident that they were merely waiting for a hopeless garrison to starve, the sentries at the guard posts would be even less on the alert. He worked out a plan that would end the isolation of the castle from his people in the settlements outside.

The Earl's army was concentrated around the castle. Beyond the sentry lines there was little risk in movement at night. By land and sea provisions could be brought up to the woods. Replacements for the garrison would give his men a well-earned rest.

The Earl was bound eventually to make some move. When winter took its grip and life in his encampment became insufferable he would launch an attack to be met by a castle refreshed with new men and well provisioned. He would never sit out there all winter when he knew that the castle and its garrison was as strong as when the siege began.

Plans for the new venture were worked out with military precision. The messengers were briefed; lists of provisions were made; meeting places selected deep in the woods. Everything was settled and ready to go when luck turned against them in a way that Swayne had least anticipated.

On the day the messengers were to leave there was a light fall of snow.

They were in November now, but snow rarely fell in those parts until after Christmas, if at all. It was no more than a sprinkling, barely covering the ground, but enough to leave tracks through the sentry lines: wide open evidence of what was going on.

'It won't lay long this time of year,' Swayne said. 'It'll probably be gone by morning and we'll start tomorrow night.'

But it didn't go. Some time around dawn there was another fall: heavier this time, and when the garrison looked out from the ramparts the surrounding fields were covered.

'I don't envy them out there in those flimsy tents,' said Swayne, but it was faint consolation for the garrison.

For weeks they had looked upon the siege as broken. Every night they had gone freely into the woods, laughing at the impotence of the enemy. The new venture had promised leave to see their families again; fresh men for the castle; food in plenty to liven up their rations. Now the snow had imprisoned them more securely than anything the Earl could have achieved.

The winter of 1216 was the worst in living memory.

There was no more snow but it steadily grew colder. Each night Swayne went to the summit of the fortress, hoping for a veering of the wind that would bring moist air from the south, but it was always the same: another bitter, ice-cold night.

Some mornings around midday they would see a pale outline of the sun behind the leaden clouds and say, 'It's breaking through. We shan't have to wait long now,' but by afternoon it had gone, with another freezing night.

They had plenty of fuel from the wood stacks around the ramparts. They kept the fortress warm with fires in the kitchen and in the hall. They kept up their evening suppers with singing and music afterwards but there was something unreal and forced about it now.

For a time they managed to keep parts of the moat open for their nets and lines by breaking the ice with iron bars. But one morning the men came back empty handed. The moat was frozen solid. There were no more fish.

And every day the cold intensified. It seemed as if the whole world was frozen.

Chapter Eleven

For the Earl the freeze-up was a gift from heaven.

The sting of winter had made his pavilion well nigh insufferable. A brazier had been installed, but it filled the place with smoke and the Earl could scarcely breathe.

When the 'deserter' had told him of the desperate condition of the garrison he had called upon his two mercenary Captains to stage an immediate assault, but Raymond and Conrad had put him off. They may have guessed that the story was a hoax to entice an attack, and argued that if the garrison was so near surrender they might as well wait for the castle to fall into their hands.

The Earl had no choice but to accept their decision and resigned himself to the dreary business of waiting for the garrison to starve, until the morning when a servant told him that the river was so deeply frozen that they had to break the ice with an axe to draw water for the camp.

The news was so exciting that the Earl forgot his chil-blained fingers and numbed feet. He called in his two mercenary Captains and said:

'You've often told me that the moat was the only obstacle to a direct assault. If the river is so deeply frozen that axes are needed to break the ice, then the still water of the moat must have frozen even deeper. Now is our chance! We must act at once! Before a thaw sets in!'

Raymond and Conrad tried to hedge. Their men were now comfortably settled in for the winter, drawing good food and pay. They argued that a military assault upon a castle had never, in their experience, been attempted under such conditions. It would be impossible to scale ramparts coated with ice.

But the Earl brushed this aside. 'The siege tower!' he shouted. 'It was useless when the moat was a barrier, but now you can thrust it across the ice, hard up against the castle ramparts!'

There wasn't any answer to this, and when the Earl promised a handsome reward for a quick victory Raymond and Conrad went off to brief their men.

It was no surprise to Swayne when he saw an ox team dragging the unwieldy tower across the snowbound fields. From the day the moat had frozen he knew that the enemy would take swift advantage of it.

'The siege tower is an open gateway to the castle,' he told his officers. 'It would be suicide to defend the ramparts against mercenaries outnumbering us ten to one. We'll make the fortress our stronghold.'

'If I had my way,' he said, 'I'd get the whole garrison safely inside the fortress before the mercenaries set foot on the ramparts, but they wouldn't take kindly to locking themselves in without attempting to hit back.'

He decided upon a small 'token force' of six men to conceal themselves behind the battlements and do what damage they could when the bridge from the siege tower was lowered on to the ramparts. It was only to be a 'token resistance'. He would watch from the fortress and sound the tocsin when he saw the men in danger of being over-whelmed. They would then race for the fortress. The steps would be drawn in and the pass door bolted. It wouldn't hold up the assault for long, but the garrison would be all the better for a few punches at the mercenaries before they went on to the defensive.

They watched the siege tower dragged slowly forward by the ox team. It was a difficult, precarious business. The snow was not deep, but sufficient to cover the rough meadowland. If a wheel dipped into a hole the tall top-heavy structure could turn right over. Men went ahead laying planks to keep the tower on a level surface. Sand was thrown down to give the oxen a safe foothold. There were frequent stops to relay the planks and Swayne reckoned that they wouldn't be ready to attack before next morning.

Meanwhile the garrison prepared the fortress as the final bulwark of resistance.

Every spare corner was stacked with logs for fuel, and all reserve supplies of arrows were brought in from the wall turrets. Nothing of any value was left outside. The enemy would find a barren waste inside the castle walls.

By nightfall the siege tower had been dragged to within a hundred yards of the frozen moat. The oxen were unharnessed and taken away. Lanterns glowed in the lower room of the siege tower where men remained on watch, and the garrison spent its last nights of duty on the ramparts.

Morning came with a pale wintry sun, no breath of wind, still freezing hard, the snow as dry as powder. Swayne had hoped until the last that the weather might come to their rescue. Heavy snow would have immobilized the siege tower: a gale could have overturned it. A few hours of thaw would have weakened the ice around the moat and made it precarious for the heavy tower.

But luck had turned against the garrison and given the Earl its blessing. The whole company of mercenaries had been assembled. With the ox teams discarded the final advance of the tower was done by manpower. Soon after dawn the advance began.

The lower part of the tower was open to the ground. Some worked inside it, pushing it forward on its wheels. Others, protected by a penthouse, pushed from behind.

It was a strange, uncanny opening to the attack. Beyond the creaking of the wheels there was no sound. Swayne, from the watch tower, could see the six men of his 'token force' crouched behind the ramparts.

When the tower had been manoeuvred to the moat the most difficult part of its journey began. There was a drop of about two feet to the frozen surface of the water. Planks were pushed forward from beneath the tower to give it a gradual way down.

The mercenaries strained at ropes to hold it back. There was a groaning of timbers as the unwieldy tower leant perilously forward in taking the decline. Then with a jolt and a rattle it stood fair and square on the frozen surface of the moat within a few feet of the castle ramparts.

Though tall and difficult to manoeuvre, the tower was lightly built. The timber framework was coated with tough leather, impervious to arrows and small missiles. Inside three platforms, one above the other, were served by ladders. The front wall of the top platform was hinged to let down as a bridge.

There was room for no more than a dozen on each platform. When the bridge was lowered the first wave would go forward from the assault platform and their places taken by men waiting below, and so the whole company would surge across the bridge.

While the mercenaries made their preparations the waiting must have seemed interminable for the six men of the 'token force' crouched behind the ramparts. For Swayne the problem had been how to arm them. Arrows would be useless at so short a range, and their own light swords were toys compared with the massive weapons of the mercenaries. Swayne had solved the problem by arming them with antique weapons that hadn't seen the light of day for years.

When the hall had been decorated somebody had discovered a bundle of old pikes, or lances, hidden away in a store shed. Where they had come from nobody knew, but they looked fine on the walls of the castle hall among the ancient shields and banners. Six feet long with sharp iron points they were just the things they needed.

At last the hinged wall of the upper platform flew open and came down with a thud on to the ramparts. It was the sound the defenders had been waiting for. They stood up behind the ramparts with their pikes gripped ready to attack. The siege tower, as a means of assault, had certain limitations. The bridge, or gangway, was only wide enough for two men abreast. Open on both sides, with no protecting rails, it would have been precarious under the best conditions. Defended by six lusty men with pikes it became, at first, a deathtrap.

The two leading attackers were giants: seemingly invincible in their armoured breast plates as they came forward with drawn swords.

They were midway across the bridge and taken completely by surprise. They were prepared for swordsmen: not devils with long poles. They tried to parry with their swords, but the powerful well-aimed blows were too much for them. Struck full in the chests they lost their balance, toppled backwards and fell off the bridge to crash on the ice-bound moat beneath them.

The next were too close behind the leaders to see what happened. All they knew was that the two giants in front came staggering back, nearly knocking them off the bridge. They were still trying to recover their balance when the pikes did the rest; two more crashes on the ice beneath, more helpless cries and agonizing groans.

The 'token force' was jubilant. For the first time they had come within striking distance of the hated mercenaries who had done such damage to their castle. It was a glorious revenge, and they stood there shouting defiance. With their long pikes it was easy to push them off the bridge. They could have done it as well with barge poles.

Watching from the summit of the fortress. Swayne was astonished by the exploits of his men. He had expected a few valiant but ineffective prods that the armoured mercenaries would have barely felt. He had never envisaged them sending the four leaders flying. He stood by the toscin, ready to signal the retreat, but held his hand. They wouldn't have forgiven him calling them back in their moment of triumph. To his lasting regret he allowed them to stay and face the next assault.

After that first ill-fated sortie the attackers had been called back into the tower. When the next appeared on the gangway they carried leather shields sent up to them from below. Swayne's men drove their pikes at them. The pikes penetrated the shields but could not be withdrawn. The two leading mercenaries were pushed bodily forward by those behind. As they fell wounded on to the ramparts they were trampled on by the crowd that came surging across the gangway, leaping on to the walls.

Swayne sounded the tocsin. Maybe in their excitement his men didn't hear it. More likely they ignored it. For months they had wanted to get to grips with the mercenaries. Their easy success with the pikes had turned their heads. When the pikes were caught in the enemy shields they couldn't swallow their pride and run like rabbits for the safety of the fortress. They drew their swords and tried to fight back.

Swayne beat the tocsin time and again, still hoping to bring his men back to their senses. But the chance of escape had gone. The mercenaries were pouring in, the defenders were surrounded.

The fate of the whole castle hung in the balance.

The rest of the garrison, at action stations in the fortress, had been elated by the exploit on the ramparts. They had raised cheers of delight when they saw the leading attackers knocked off the bridge.

And when the tables turned: when suddenly they saw their friends outnumbered, fighting for their lives, their only thought was to go to their rescue. Discipline was thrown to the winds. They left their stations at the embrasures: drew their swords and began crowding down the turret steps to the doorway leading to the ramparts.

Swayne faced a cruel decision. To stop them going to the rescue, to bolt the fortress door and leave their stricken friends outside seemed, at that moment, a craven desire to save their own skins at the expense of the men fighting so valiantly on the ramparts. There was no time for Swayne to explain that the men were already beyond help, that if the garrison deserted the fortress in a suicidal attempt at rescue the fate of the castle would be sealed. All that could be said late – if the time ever came. But now the only shield against disaster was stark brutality.

In a blazing fury he forced his way down the turret steps, thrusting the men aside. 'Get back to your stations!' he shouted. 'How dare you leave them without orders!'

The door stood open, the ladder still down to receive the 'token force' had they responded to the signal to retreat. Two guards stood ready to draw the ladder in when the men outside returned.

They were hesitating: wondering what to do. They would no doubt have stood aside and let the garrison go through if Swayne had not forced his way in front of them.

'Draw the ladder up!' he shouted.

He stood with his back to the open door, blocking the way as the garrison came surging round, struggling to get through.

'You heard my order! Get back to your stations! You are here to save the castle! Not to throw it away!'

Swayne's quiet methods in the past were the saving of the situation now. The men had never seen him in this towering rage before. They stood there astonished and subdued, like a herd of stampeding cattle suddenly facing a brick wall. Bernard took over: the burly second in command who was called 'the bull'. He bellowed at the men like an outraged sergeant-major. 'You heard the Commander's orders – get back to your stations and do your jobs! Go on! Get back!' And the men, shocked back to obedience and discipline, returned to the embrasures of the fortress.

Things had happened so quickly that barely ten minutes had passed since the mercenaries had attacked from the siege tower.

It had been a blitzkrieg. In that short time they had stormed the ramparts and captured the whole outer defences of the castle.

Raymond had directed the assault from the siege tower. He now crossed the bridge and looked around him. For months he had watched the castle from a distance. He now saw for the first time the barrenness and frugality of it: a few wooden shacks – roofs shattered by the missiles; a broken target used for practice; the ruins of a field kitchen: nothing else on the churned up land but the central fortress that stood there silent and apparently derelict, scarred and pockmarked by the long bombardment.

What lay inside? A few men, too weak from starvation to take part in that last, despairing effort? A few victims of the bombardment maimed and crippled. Though hardened by professional warfare, Raymond felt respect for a valiant enemy, pity for them in defeat. He was not looking forward to exploring that shattered citadel, to what he would discover in its twilit rooms and passages.

He chose a dozen men to go with him. 'If any are still alive,' he said: 'then carry them out and give them food and wine. The Earl will expect some prisoners, especially the Commander and his son.

The Earl's own son is probably in the dungeon. He must be treated with respect and conducted back to his father at once.'

What was inside the fortress they soon discovered.

They were half way across the open land when one of the mercenaries fell with a groan, clutching at an arrow in his chest. It was the first of a storm of arrows that came from every embrasure of the fortress that faced their advance.

The garrison had held their hands until the mercenaries were well out in the open, away from the protection of the siege tower. Four fell in the first volley. They had harely recovered form their surprise when a second volley brought down three more. Raymond felt a searing pain in his right arm. He dragged the arrow from the sleeve of his torn tunic and shouted: 'Back!'

The survivors didn't stop until they reached cover in the siege tower. And all the way more arrows whistled past them, with cheers of exultation from the fortress.

Chapter Twelve

As Raymond stood in the siege tower with a man binding the painful flesh wound in his arm he faced the even more painful fact that, far from over, the assault had only just begun. How many of the garrison had survived to hold the fortress he couldn't tell, but judging by that storm of arrows, the hard core remained untouched, and very much alive.

New plans weren't going to be easy. The fortress stood centrally within the surrounding ramparts. The open ground around it was now a 'no-man's-land' commanded on all sides by bowmen safely installed behind embrasures in the fortress walls. The surrounding ramparts were a hindrance rather than a help. They naturally faced outwards, against an attacking enemy. On the inner side was an open path in full view of the fortress: the outer wall dropped sheer to the moat. The only safe place to keep watch was from the siege tower. They were back where they had started.

So far as watch was concerned, little was needed. The garrison wasn't likely to make a sortie. Raymond's problem was to capture the fortress and get hold of the elusive garrison. A massed attack would get nowhere. The only entrance to the fortress was by a narrow door well above ground level, now closed and barred, with the ladder withdrawn. An attempt to break in with scaling ladders would expose them to the arrows of the garrison shot point blank from a dozen embrasures in the walls. The fortress was like a gigantic oyster without a cleft in it to force it open.

New plans would have to wait. Raymond's first job was to report to the Earl and tell him what had happened.

It wasn't a pleasant meeting.

The Earl exploded in a fury. It was enough to drive him raving mad. He was sick with cold. The braziers filled his pavilion with suffocating smoke. He could scarcely breathe when he went to bed. The frozen moat had been the godsend he had prayed for. The castle was at his mercy. Swayne and his son would soon hang from the ramparts and he would return as victor to the comfort of his castle. And now this accursed Raymond calmly told him that they were no nearer to the end than ever.

'You told me on your word of honour that you would have the castle in your hands by nightfall! With the whole surviving garrison my prisoners!'

'I said nothing of the sort,' retorted Raymond. 'I carried out your instructions and invaded from the siege tower. We succeeded in that completely, but none of us could tell what the enemy would do.'

'Why didn't you storm the fortress before they shut themselves in?'

'Because,' replied Raymond: 'they had drawn up the ladder and barred the door before we had crossed the outer ramparts.'

'Then get them out! Get them out!' shouted the Earl. He was purple in the face, trembling with rage. 'If you value your reputation as a soldier you will capture that accursed fortress in the next few days. If you fail, then I shall make it known all over Europe, and you will be disgraced. I shall see that you are not worth a . . .' and the Earl was overcome by the wrenching, agonizing cough that had haunted him for days. He staggered into his pavilion, leaving Raymond standing outside in the snow.

Raymond shrugged his shoulders and walked away. He was miserable and frightened. He knew that the Earl had the power to carry out his threats. The wound in his arm was throbbing painfully, bleeding through its bandages. He had been up all night and longed to lie down and rest, but he had to go back and work out a plan to make a final breakthrough into that accursed fortress.

When the bombardment had reached its climax and the fortress had seemed doomed. Swayne had planned to evacuate the castle:

break through the enemy cordon by night and organize a new resistance in the nearest fishing village with their backs to the sea.

He regretted now that he had let the chance go by. With an open way by sea they could have brought in food and reinforcements. The village was practically surrounded by the marshes, impossible for the enemy to attack. Their boats would have come freely to and fro. So long as they held out the Earl would not be master of their land. With the whole of the Swayne people supporting them, they could never have been defeated.

But all those rosy dreams were gone. They were imprisoned now with no escape. The men were in good heart. They had revenged the death of their friends and the fortress was impregnable. The mercenaries, for the first time, were on the defensive. The garrison hoped that they would attack again, to be mowed down by arrows.

But the Earl in fact held all the cards. With his mercenaries surrounding the fortress in a stranglehold, he could send most of his levies home. Swayne's hope of the Earl's defeat through lack of money went for nothing now. The cost of the mercenaries alone would be well within his pocket for months to come.

The question now was not for how long the Earl could hold out. It was for how long the garrison could hold out under the new conditions.

Thanks to the rabbit snaring they had not drawn much upon the food in store. It was less a matter of how long the food would last, as for how long they would have the fuel to cook it. In the vaults they had sufficient provisions to last about six weeks, but salted meat, dried beans and grain had to be cooked. They had stacked the fortress with all the logs they had room for, but logs, without peat to smoulder with them, burnt ravenously. Stacked against the ramparts were enough logs to last for months: so near and yet so far. They couldn't go out and get them beneath the very noses of the mercenaries.

'How long would you give our fuel to last?' asked Swayne.

Father Peter said about three weeks, if the cooks kept the fires down to a smoulder.

For a few days the new conditions beguiled the men and then

the old enemy, stagnation, raised its head. They began to think longingly of the days when they had the freedom of the castle, target practice outside, and above all those nights of foraging in the woods. Cooped up in the twilit fortress told upon their nerves.

They saw no sign of the enemy beyond occasional furtive shadows at the windows of the siege tower. 'If only they would come out and fight!' they said. But the mercenaries weren't there to provide sitting targets for the bowmen at the embrasures. Swayne kept up the evening dinner in the hall, with the lamps alight around the walls, and music and singing afterwards, but the men would go back to their quarters in silence, to another dark winter night.

It was the enemy who shook the garrison out of their stagnation.

One night they heard a resounding crash. It was very dark and it wasn't until daybreak that they found out what had happened. During the bombardment they had taken the chains and cables from the drawbridge to support the padding against the fortress wall. The mercenaries now wanted to use the bridge, but having no means of lowering it had cut the remaining supports and let it come down with a crash.

It was also clear why they had done it. They had brought up a dozen penthouses and were wheeling them across the bridge, lashing them together and pushing them forward across the open land towards the fortress. Their scheme was clear enough. With the doorway of the fortress beyond their reach they had decided to thrust their penthouses against the wall and break through at ground level.

The garrison had twice seen the penthouses in use and had no answer to them. The steep sloping roofs made arrows and small missiles useless. The men inside could wheel them forward in perfect safety. Some of them came labouring across the drawbridge with a heavy ram that had a vicious iron point to it, and slung it inside the leading penthouses.

As they came slowly forward Swayne did some rapid thinking. A breakthrough at ground level would lead the mercenaries into the storeroom, now almost empty. In the vaults beneath were stacked the old tattered buffers that had served to fend off the bombardment.

They were dragged up into the storeroom and packed against the wall that the mercenaries would soon be breaking down. Behind the buffers were the sleeping mattresses: all the old rope and sacking they could lay their hands on: piles of logs and bags of debris. By the time they had finished the storeroom was packed solid from floor to ceiling. It was a race against time: urged on by the concussions of the ram against the wall outside.

The wall at its base was faced with blocks of iron-hard stone. For a while the ram made little impression but when the outer stones were loosened the sharp point of the ram drove easily into the core of smaller stones. A line of men beneath the penthouses handed back the debris to keep the passage clear, and at last the driving point was through.

They still had to widen the gap for the men to get through. They were prepared for a desperate last ditch resistance from the garrison, but at close quarters, with their heavy swords, they could soon cut down the defenders and have the fortress in their hands.

Then came the unexpected setback. When the final blows of the ram had done their work the attackers were not faced by the expected armed resistance but by a spongy mass of old twisted cowhides, an evil-smelling jumble of knotted ropes and chains and logs, tattered sacks and horsehair mattresses.

Raymond came forward to investigate. 'We've broken through into an old rubbish dump,' he said: 'push it away! Get it out!'

The men began pulling out the stuff in handfuls: they dug into it with swords and daggers, but the deeper they went the harder it was to pull out. When the tight-packed stuff was loosened, it regained its normal bulk. The front penthouse was soon full of it. The mercenaries gathered it up and passed it back, but it was an endless business. A mattress almost filled the penthouse. They had to tear it up before they could get rid of it.

Raymond lost his temper. A lot of old cowhides and rubbish holding up an elite corps of mercenaries: the finest soldiers in Europe! It was humiliating! It wasn't war!

'Push it out of the way with the ram!' he shouted.

But the ram only made things worse. It merely squashed into

the rubbish and packed it tighter. It was the story of the bombardment over again. The granite missiles could smash the stone walls of a fortress but were useless against cushions of straw-filled hides. The iron-pointed ram could cleave through a solid five foot wall of stone, but was beaten by a squashy mass of rubbish.

Meanwhile the garrison had been busy overhead. The small missiles on the summit of the fortress were useless against the tough sloping walls of the penthouses, but there was a weapon far more potent and devastating if they could make use of it in time.

The front penthouse, under which the mercenaries were working, stood firm against the fortress wall. Surrounding the summit of the fortress was a parapet of stone. The masons got busy driving wedges around a section of the parapet that weighed at least a ton.

They crowded around the loosened slab and strained it back and forth to break down the remaining cement that held it. When finally it gave way the whole massive chunk fell with a resounding crash, full on to the penthouse roof.

When the cloud of dust subsided the scene below was chaos. The penthouse had been smashed to pieces. The mercenaries beneath it lay spreadeagled on all sides: some stunned or dead: some feebly trying to crawl away. The ram lay half buried by the massive stones of the fallen parapet. The whole area was covered by a shambles of old cowhides and rubbish that the mercenaries had pulled out of the hole.

Raymond, who had barely escaped himself, shouted to the men in the penthouses behind to thrust them forward to replace the one that had been shattered. While they were exposed the garrison bombarded them with hand missiles as they cleared the debris and dragged the bodies of their dead and wounded to one side.

By now the garrison was scenting victory. It wasn't difficult, with crowbars, to break loose another chunk of the parapet and lever it into position above the second penthouse. This time the mercenaries got warning. A watchman saw the garrison straining at the slab and shouted to the men. They scrambled back into the penthouses behind and were clear before the slab crashed down.

It killed no men, but crushed the second penthouse to pieces, leaving no cover to work against the fortress wall.

Raymond had had enough. It was something he couldn't fight back against. He had been prepared for arrows and small missiles that the penthouses could parry, but had never envisaged the garrison hacking away slabs of their own fortress to smash the penthouses like eggshells.

The attempt to break in with the ram had been forced upon him by the Earl. The only alternatives were tunnelling or fire. He could tunnel under the foundations and break in from below. But that would be an enormous labour, taking months. He could build stacks of wood around the fortress, set them afire and burn or smoke the defenders out. But the stacks would have to be built in full view of the defenders: a harvest for their bowmen. And with ample water from their well they could put the fires out even if the stacks were built.

The breakthrough with the ram had been the only possibility. The chances had been good, but they had failed. Raymond ordered the assault party to retire under cover of the remaining penthouses, back to the safety of the archway beneath the gatehouse.

What he said to the Earl, and what the Earl said to him needs no recording.

Chapter Thirteen

The garrison could chalk up another victory if they chose, but it had got them nowhere.

At first they believed that the Earl had made his final throw. Driven by the insufferable cold he had made that ferocious attack out of sheer desperation, but it seemed that the Earl was impervious to defeat. The mercenaries kept up their stranglehold around the fortress and the levies continued to man the guard tents as an outer defence.

All day the garrison could hear the thud of axes in the woodlands where the enemy were felling trees for their camp fires. There wasn't a sign that the Earl had the least intention of giving up. He had evidently returned to the unfailing weapon of starvation. There was still one hope for the garrison, if it came in time. The Earl was dependent for all his supplies upon the solitary road that crossed the downs. If a heavy fall of snow were to block this road it would cut off his provisions and bring his army to starvation. With hundreds of men out there in the freezing cold the end of their food supply would spread disaster.

For weeks the garrison had prayed for the weather to break. They now prayed for the freeze to remain, for a massive snowfall to besiege and destroy the enemy. The freeze remained but the snow never came, and the garrison could only watch the convoys of supply wagons arriving daily in the enemy camp.

To eke out their fuel supply they unravelled the stuffing in the storeroom that had stopped the mercenaries from breaking in. There wasn't much likelihood of another attack, and they used the old cowhides and sacks for the kitchen fire. The stuff made a foul smell but it kept the fire smouldering during the night.

With the last of the logs they made one final roaring fire and cooked the remaining meat in store. They put in the dried peas and beans, boiled the whole lot together and stored it in earthen jars. They pounded the grain to bake bread, and that night the fire sank down and died.

Swayne and his officers talked between themselves of surrender but the time for that had long since passed. They had twice rejected the Earl's offer. To surrender now would only mean walking out to be hanged. Father Peter, as priest and confessor, rejected the idea of telling the men they were doomed. 'I don't intend,' he said, 'to deliver a funeral oration over men still alive. Let them keep a shred of hope until the end. I shall pray for their salvation but shall do it privately, without disturbing them, and when their time comes, the cold will make the passing merciful.'

Father Peter was in no doubt right. The garrison never gave up hope. They continued their sentry duties at the embrasures: always hoping to see the enemy camp break up against the merciless cold.

The fortress, without fires, became an ice-house. In the stagnant, twilit passages there was no means for exercise. To give the men fresh air and a sight of the open sky Swayne sent them by rotation to the summit of the fortress, but for men near starving an hour up there in the bitter wind was as much as they could endure. Their only relief was to huddle in their blankets, close together for warmth. Their one remaining consolation lay in their pride in denying the Earl his final victory.

One morning Father Peter said to Swayne, 'I can eke out the remaining food to last three days, but the men find it revolting. It makes them sick to put those frozen lumps into their mouths. So why not make a fire and have one good hot meal to finish up with?'

'A fire?' asked Swayne. 'From what?'

'From the tables and the wooden stools,' said Father Peter. 'From the wooden cupboard in my room, from the framework of the catapult on the watch tower, even the ladder from the pass door to the ground. We shan't need these things any longer. Lit from the flame of our solitary lamp they'd make a fine blaze in the hearth of the hall. We'd break those last jars of frozen food, put it all in a stew pot and have one final hot supper to warm the heart. Does it sound too much like a funeral feast? Even so, why not?'

'Why not?' said Swayne. 'I'll leave you to tell the men why we're doing it because it'll come best from you.'

Father Peter put it to the men in his own special way. He had reserved some wine in a cask in the vault, he said. They would all have a drink to prepare them for their journey and he would go with them to see them safely through the golden gates.

The men understood. Their trust in the old priest was absolute. He would be with them on that final adventure as he had been with them from the day they were born, and what better way to prepare for the journey than with a good hot meal and a glass of wine. 'Your families will not suffer,' he told them. 'They will know what you did to remain undefeated, and even if the Earl holds sway over them for a little while, they will remember you, and be the victors in the end.'

But the 'funeral feast' never happened, for reasons that Father Peter had never contemplated.

It was late in the morning of that final day when they saw a solitary man coming slowly down the hill side from the Earl's pavilion. He was old, and walked slowly with a painful limp. He carried a long staff to help him on his way and was shrouded against the cold in a hooded cloak. He came slowly across the drawbridge and stopped beneath the archway for a word with the mercenaries on duty there. Then he came on alone across the open land towards the fortress.

Whoever he was, Swayne admired his courage. He carried no arms or shield. They could easily have shot him down. Swayne stayed their hands and waited. When he saw the defenders on the summit of the fortress he raised a hand in a diffident, uncertain way, a kind of shy salute.

'I come in peace,' he said. 'I wish to speak with Lord Swayne, your Commander.'

Swayne hesitated. Was it another of the Earl's crafty tricks – an old man seeking entrance to the fortress under cover of his age? If they lowered the steps to let him in, would it be the signal for a hoard of mercenaries to come surging out of hiding places?

'I can hear you,' said Swayne. 'You can tell me what you have to say from where you are.'

The old man stood in silence for a while, then raised his head and said, 'I give you my word of honour that I come in peace. I cannot tell you what I have to say unless I can speak intimately with you.'

Swayne couldn't resist pity for him, standing out there in the bitter cold. If he were in fact a decoy then he was a consummate actor. He looked so pathetic with his grey, haggard face and trembling hands, yet brave to stand there exposed to the arrows of the garrison.

'Wait there,' said Swayne, 'until I can arrange for you to come in.'

Taking no chances he stationed bowmen at the embrasures, then ordered the door to be unbolted and the steps to be let down.

The old man had difficulty in climbing the steep steps. Two of Swayne's officers went down to help him. They assisted him into the hall and gave him a seat at the table.

The climb had exhausted him. He sat back in his chair, breathing with difficulty.

'I am sorry . . .' he said in a low voice. 'This . . . this weakness . . . I cannot help . . .'

Swayne had no more suspicions of a trick, or subterfuge. The old man was clearly very weak and ill. Father Peter gave him some of their remaining wine.

He drank a little, said, 'Thank you . . . thank you,' and lay back in his chair.

'You must forgive me,' he said. 'I hoped to conceal my weakness . . . but the walk across the fields . . . it was very difficult . . .' He lowered his head and muttered to himself, as if trying to collect his thoughts and put them into words.

Presently he glanced up at the men around the table and said, 'I am the Earl's Chancellor, his Treasurer and Chancellor. He has always granted me authority to act on his behalf . . .' He drew aside his cloak and groped with a trembling hand for a little badge hung on a thin gold chain around his neck: a beautiful little miniature of the Earl's coat of arms.

'This is my token of authority,' he said.

'And what has the Earl instructed you to say?' asked Swayne.

The old man passed a trembling hand across his eyes, 'I came to inform you,' he replied, 'that the Earl is dead.'

Swayne's officers around the table exchanged knowing, sidelong glances. 'So here's the trick,' they seemed to say. 'He's here to tell us this to make us cheer and go outside to be shot down by the mercenaries!' If he had told them that the world would end that night they couldn't have been less believing. To them the Earl had become a symbol of devilish hostility, merciless and indestructible. To be told that he was human enough to die was an insult to their understanding.

But the old man was talking on. 'The Earl was a big stalwart man,' he said, 'but he was poor in health. He should never, at his age, have undertaken the ardours of this siege. He had not foreseen the difficulties and anxieties of it. But he had great power of will. He carried on until the cold was more than his weakened body could withstand, and this morning, when his servants went to the pavilion, they found him dead.'

It sounded convincing enough, but Swayne's officers still hesitated. They were thinking of those beguiling invitations to 'walk out in honourable peace' to be cut down, like as not, the moment they had left the castle.

The old man seemed to know what they were thinking.

'If you doubt my word,' he said, 'then look for yourselves. When I reached the castle I told the men on duty that the Earl was dead, that the siege was over and they were to return to camp. The commanders of levies are making their own arrangements for departure. If you will look, you will know that I am not deceiving you.'

They went to a window, and there, sure enough, was the confirmation they required. The mercenaries had left their guard posts. Their military precision had gone. They were wandering away towards their encampment in little groups of two and threes. In the encampment beside the river they saw the tents being lowered, carpenters dismantling the wooden huts, wagons being loaded up.

'You may wonder why we have discarded the siege so abruptly,' said the old man, 'so quickly after the Earl's death . . . We do so in no confession of defeat. Had the Earl lived we would have stood by him until the end, for that was our bounden duty. But his death released us from our bond. The Earl, and the Earl alone, desired this campaign against you. As his chief counsellor I did my best to dissuade him. I did not believe in the justice of it. But the Earl was adamant. It had become an obsession with him, and we as his servants had to obey.'

'All that I accept,' said Swayne. 'But there are things that go much deeper. The Earl persuaded King John that I was a traitor and received a Royal warrant to capture this castle in his name. If the Earl died only a few hours ago, you have clearly not had time to inform the King and receive his instructions to abandon the siege. What right have you to countermand Royal orders? King John presumably still thinks I am a traitor. How am I to know that he will not hand the warrant to another baron to carry on this siege in the Earl's place?'

The old man looked baffled. He was very tired and found it difficult to explain. 'I am sorry,' he said. 'Confined to this castle you have not heard what all men in this island have known for many days. King John was on his way north when he caught a fever one autumn night and died at Newark Abbey. His son, a boy of thirteen, is now the king, with a Regency Council to govern for him. The warrant granted to the Earl became void at the King's death, and the Council, who seek only peace, are unlikely to revive it.'

'And yet,' said Swayne, 'when the Earl knew that the King was dead, and that his warrant had expired, he continued the siege as if nothing had happened?'

The old Chancellor raised his hands in helpless despair. Why could this suspicious man not understand?

'I have already told you,' he replied. 'The capture of this castle was an obsession with the Earl. Nothing could divert him from it.'

Swayne looked out across the snowbound fields. The mercenaries had gone. The guard tents that had surrounded the castle since the siege began were being rolled up and tossed into a wagon.

'You can see for yourself,' said the Chancellor, 'his army is on the march, delighted to be going home.'

He had risen from his chair and limped across to Swayne.

'There is one matter,' he said, 'that concerns me very greatly. Before this siege began, the Earl's son Gregory fell into your hands. We had no news, no word concerning what you . . . what you . . .' He hesitated, and Swayne helped him out.

'What we had done with him? You need have no fears on that. We have held the boy captive in this castle. He has behaved himself well and shared our difficulties. But he is alive and in good health.'

A look of such relief came into the old Chancellor's face that it seemed as if the burden of his years had dropped from him. He was alert, excited, and began for the first time to talk without restraint.

'I am delighted!' he said. 'Most grateful to you for your care of him! I must tell you, between ourselves, that the Earl had no liking for Gregory. It may sound brutal, but he would not have been sorry if the boy had perished in the bombardment of this castle. He was rebellious and disobedient and the Earl had a younger son whom he liked better. But all of us, except the Earl, preferred the elder boy. He is far more worthy to succeed, and it is a joy to us that he has survived!'

The old man calmed down. Delicate negotiations lay ahead. He was now the shrewd, hard-headed man of business who had taken such care of the Earl's money bags.

'It is usual,' he said, 'to pay ransom for the return of a distinguished captive. That we shall gladly do. But you will know, of course, that the cost of this campaign has made great inroads upon the fortunes of the Earl's estates . . .'

As he listened to the old man trying to soften up the ransom, it occurred to Swayne what reparations he could claim if he had a mind to it. The old humbug was pleading for extenuations on account of what the siege had cost the Earl! What in heaven's name did he think it had cost the Swaynes? Gregory was in their power. The Earl's army had dispersed. Nothing on earth would bring them back to begin the siege again. He could demand a massive ransom: he could name his own price.

But that would need bluff, and Swayne wasn't good at bluff. The old Chancellor's intervention that day had saved the garrison from certain starvation. They had in fact planned to send Gregory back to the Earl's camp that afternoon, before their final 'funeral feast'.

Swayne wanted no money. All the money the Chancellor could pay would not bring back the men that Swayne had lost, nor repair the damage to his domain. All he wanted now was the freedom to put right what could only be done with their own hands: by their own ceaseless work.

'I want no ransom for the boy,' he said. 'He is free to return with you at once.'

While the old man was still muttering his incredulous thanks and gratitude Swayne went to the door and called for Roger. He took the boy aside and told him what had happened.

'I think you would like to break the news to Gregory yourself,' he said. 'When you have explained things to him, bring him down here and we will say goodbye.'

As Roger went up the turret steps to the room that he had shared with Gregory his thoughts ran back to the first day when he had tried to make friends with him: when Gregory had insulted him and Roger had gone back to his father in a fury and said, 'Put him in the dungeon to teach him a lesson.'

He would never have thought the day would come to say goodbye to Gregory as a friend. It had happened so gradually that he could never have said when he had ceased to loathe him and begun to like him. It had started when Gregory had been given freedom to walk with Roger around the ramparts. They had nothing in common.

They had come from different worlds. At first they walked in silence, a jailer with a prisoner at exercise. Slowly they had discovered things to talk about, obvious things like the gulls overhead, a rabbit bolting across a field, the gathering of thunder clouds or the ebb and flow of the tides in the nearby estuary. Such casual talk broke down the barriers.

During the bombardment when Gregory had been kept to his room, Roger would put his plate on the tray containing Gregory's dinner and take it up so that they could eat together. Afterwards they would play chess in the light of their solitary lantern. When there was no oil to spare for their lantern they would move the table into the embrasure and play their games in the moonlight that filtered through the narrow window, or in the fitful glimmer of the stars. Their eyes became accustomed to the darkness. Then they would stretch out on their mattresses and yarn together until they talked themselves to sleep.

In the final days, when the fuel ran out and the fortress was bitterly cold, they devised ways of seeing the night through without being frozen in their beds. They gave up sleeping on separate mattresses, put one above the other like a sandwich, and slept between them. Beforehand they would exercise, wrestle together to get their circulation up, then crawl between the mattresses, pull over their blankets and a few old tattered cowhides.

Close together for warmth, no barriers lay between them any longer. The difference in their lives that once made talk so plodding now gave them endless things to tell each other. Gregory would tell of grand occasions in his father's castle: of when King John himself had come with a magnificent retinue, and there were pageants and banquets and tournaments, and the hunting of stags and wild boar in the forests. He would tell Roger of travels with his father around their vast domains: of cities and cathedrals and a magnificent Royal castle beside the river Thames. For Roger they were like fairy stories, but he could listen for hours because Gregory would always spice them with anecdotes that had a funny side to them. He had a sly sense of humour that saw through his father's pomposity and love of show.

Roger's stories were simple and unexciting in comparison but Gregory would listen because they told him about the lives and doings of people he had never been in touch with. They were stories of the fields and woods and sea, of the way people lived in a small country town. For long hours of the winter nights the two boys lay together, son of a great Earl, son of a small country squire, sometimes hand in hand for warmth.

And now it was over. It had ended so strangely that Roger still found it difficult to believe. With all its hardships and privations he had never lost the romantic vision of a final decisive battle that would send a vanquished enemy flying for their lives. He felt that they had been cheated of the victory they had fought so hard for, but what hurt most was saying goodbye to his friend.

Gregory was standing at the window, looking out across the snow-covered fields to the distant encampment by the river.

'What's going on?' he asked. 'They're pulling down the tents and loading up the wagons. What's happened?'

Roger told him. Gregory listened in silence. He showed little surprise, and no emotion. When Roger had finished, he nodded and said, 'Well . . . we shan't be playing our game of chess tonight.'

There was something in the way he spoke that told Roger that the curtain had come down between them. The chess was over, everything was over, bar the memories.

Gregory began to unfasten the leather tunic that Roger had lent him when winter had come. 'You need this back,' he said.

'Keep it,' said Roger. 'And the woollen shirt and trunks. You can't go out on a day like this in the clothes you came in.'

'I'll send you something in return,' said Gregory, and for the first time he smiled.

They went along the narrow passage, down the winding steps into the hall.

The old Chancellor came forward, knelt painfully on one knee, took Gregory's hand and said, 'My Lord, I thank God that you are safe.'

Gregory said, 'Thank you, my good Chancellor,' and helped the old man to rise.

Watching the little ceremony, Roger could not help thinking of the nights when Gregory had poked fun at his father's love of etiquette and ceremonial. And now he was accepting it in the manner born.

The parting was soon over. Gregory thanked Swayne and his officers for their courtesy towards him. He turned to the old priest and said, rather unexpectedly, 'Give me your blessing, Father.' He knelt with lowered head and Father Peter raised his tired old hands and did as he was bid.

Gregory turned last to Roger, took his hand and said, 'We shall meet again.'

Roger stood watching Gregory as he walked slowly away beside the old limping man. Would they ever meet again? What sort of meeting could it be?

If Gregory were to ask him to visit that magnificent castle in the valley beyond the hills he would feel like an awkward rustic, lost in the grandeur of it. If Gregory were to pay a visit to their modest homespun town, they would find nothing to say to one another beyond a few polite and fatuous greetings.

Better, maybe, to bring the curtain down and leave the memories untarnished. The siege, and the upheavals of the civil war had altered nothing. Great earls would strut the land again and have more wars and rebellions in their eternal lust for power. People like the Swaynes would carry on in their own quiet, patient way, hoping only to be left alone.

Chapter Fourteen

The siege was over and the castle free, but there was no jubilation. No throwing of caps into the air. Four months of tension couldn't be peeled off and tossed aside like a worn out shirt. Guard duties had become so engrained that some of the men wandered back to the embrasures. Others stood aimlessly around, wondering whether they were awake or dreaming.

Swayne knew that it wasn't the time for a 'victory speech' or any sort of declamation that they weren't prepared for. They had got to find their own ways back to normal life again, and he did what he could to help them relax by calling them together and talking to them as if what had just happened was merely another unexpected twist in affairs that had to be coped with and straightened out.

'There's nothing to keep us here now,' he said. 'If you like we can go back to the town at once but it'll soon be dark and it'd take hours to open up the houses and get fires lit. If you ask me I'd sooner spend a final night in this old fortress and pack up in the morning. We've got enough food for one good meal. We were going to burn the furniture to cook it but there's plenty of wood in the stack outside and nobody to stop us from getting it. We can light fires and sleep warm after a good hot meal. Are you with me on that?'

They were with him to a man. Like the crew of an old storm-torn ship that had carried them safely through a perilous voyage they felt a sudden warm affection for it now that they were safe in harbour.

'Then let's get the wood for the fires,' Swayne said.

They hadn't set foot on solid earth since the mercenaries swarmed across the ramparts and imprisoned them a month ago, and like sailors after a long voyage, it took them time to find their land legs. In the cramped rooms and narrow corridors they had developed a crouched shuffling walk. When they came out into the open they still took small paces and hunched their shoulders until they were accustomed to walking upright and striding out.

When they had taken the logs to the fortress they searched the guard posts deserted by the mercenaries and found some useful booty. The mercenaries had never lacked for food and had left behind some hunks of bread and joints of meat and lanterns full of oil.

From the ramparts they watched the last of the enemy tents pulled down and loaded up. Small groups of levies were struggling along the road on their way home: their leaders on horseback beside them. It was twilight but they would march all through the winter night in their longing to get home.

All that remained standing was the Earl's pavilion with two wagons beside it. One was being loaded up with furnishings. The other stood empty until some men came out of the pavilion carrying a stretcher on which something lay, covered with the Earl's banner. When all was done the small cortège left, a groom leading the Earl's white charger behind the wagon in which his body lay. The men of the garrison saw the workmen hauling the pavilion down and remembered the summer evening when the Earl had arrived in all his glory, and how he had entertained his officers to a sumptuous banquet with music playing and his banner flying proudly overhead.

It was dark when they got back to the fortress. The lanterns had been lit. Fires were blazing in the kitchen and in the hall. An appetizing smell of cooking drifted up the kitchen steps. The meat purloined from the enemy guard posts gave flavour to the meal. Father Peter had crained the last dregs from the wine casks and mixed in some hot water to make a toddy.

For the first time since the siege began the whole garrison sat down together. No need for sentries on the ramparts any more, no worry about another freezing night. It was quieter than the make-believe 'victory suppers' because this time it was real. The men were thinking of seeing their families next day; the farmers of walking around their land; the fishermen of running their boats down to the sea again; the tradesmen of unearthing the tools that they had hidden from the enemy.

Out of the quiet moonlit night there came one sudden, unexpected alarm. An ominous rumble and crunching thud against the wall outside set them thinking that the ghost of the Earl had sent over a final spectral missile as a last gesture of defiance. But it turned out to be a chunk of frozen snow dislodged from the summit of the fortress by the warmth of the fires inside.

Swayne talked to them of the days ahead. They all knew that it wasn't to be a triumphal return to a life of bliss and plenty. The work of the settlement had come to a standstill when the Earl had invaded their territory. The harvest had been cut green or left rotting in the fields. No autumn seeding had been done. The snowfall and hard frost would have frozen the root crops in the ground and the farms would have been hard put to to keep their cattle alive.

'But we are past midwinter now,' he said. 'The sun will get warm and the land will soften. We'll plant early crops and harvest the roots. In the meantime our people won't starve. There are plenty of fish in the sea and rabbits in the woods, and out there in the forests we'll go hunting for wild hogs.'

He could have laid on the coming hardships in double measure without dampening the spirits of the men. To them it was a challenge. They had beaten the Earl and could beat the devastation he had left behind.

They brought their mattresses up from the guardroom and laid them around in the warmth of the fire. For the first time in weeks they pulled their jackets and boots off, and most of them were soon asleep.

Roger was the only restless one that night. Before settling down he went out of the fortress and walked around the deserted ramparts. He would have given a lot to have Gregory with him to share a last walk together. He told himself that he was a fool to think of

Gregory any more. It wasn't likely that Gregory was thinking about him as he rode home through the night to the great castle in the valley where there would be festivities to celebrate his succession to the earldom with streams of retainers coming in to pay him homage.

Roger had many friends among the boys in his father's small domain, but they had grown up together and shared the same ways of life. They could only talk of things that were common knowledge to them all. Gregory had opened the gates to fields of infinite adventure and discovery, but Roger had only glimpsed them from the distance and when Gregory had shaken his hand that day and said, 'We shall meet again,' it was only another way of saying goodbye.

He remembered the days that now seemed so long ago, when with the other boys they had played at defending the castle against imaginary foes. It had been great fun, and the boys would expect Roger to bring them to the castle and tell them of his exploits in the siege. That too might be great fun for the others, but for Roger there would be no more games of make-believe. With all its trials and sufferings and days upon the edge of defeat it had been a great adventure.

Sometimes in the night a man would get up to throw a few logs on to the fire. Others would stir from their sleep and by force of habit wonder whether it was time to go on duty at the watch tower, and then, remembering, would go to sleep again.

By dawn they were up and packing their belongings. The cooks made a breakfast of what was left from the night before, and having eaten they slung their packs across their shoulders and went down the fortress steps for the last time.

As they crossed the enclosure that had been a 'no-man's-land' some may have remembered the summer day when they had come into the castle and closed the gates with the distant dust clouds rising above the advancing army. The enclosure was then a lush green pasture with the cattle grazing and the poultry pecking around. Now it was a desolate waste churned up by the enemy missiles:

Littered with the wreckage of the penthouses, and debris dragged out by the mercenaries in their final effort to break in. A few granite projectiles from the trebuchets showed above the frozen snow.

When they crossed the drawbridge they were on land that they hadn't walked in daylight since the siege began. They remembered the night when they carried their wounded on the hazardous journey to the fishing boats, and the times when they had crawled through the long grass on their rabbit-snaring expeditions in the woods.

They passed the siege tower, so monstrous and menacing when the oxen had drawn it forward to the ramparts. Nothing fearsome about it now: a tall lopsided pile of scaffolding with tattered strips of leather hanging from it, deserted and forlorn.

They stopped to look at one of the massive trebuchets that had come so near to destroying the fortress, and what they saw explained the mystery of their sudden silence when victory had been almost in their hands. They saw the frayed ropes and broken cables, the cogs of the lifting wheel worn almost flat; the cracks in the crossbeam with the shooting arm leaning crazily against it. On the floor of the emplacement lay a heap of the granite missiles, ready for shooting but never used. They saw now how near they had been to disaster.

They came to a trampled circle of straw where one of the watch tents had been, and saw the narrow beaten path that the levies had made in their ceaseless patrol from tent to tent. It stretched in an unbroken circle around the castle, a dark brown girdle in the snow.

At the fringe of the woodlands they looked back at the deserted castle. From a distance it looked no different from when the siege began. The ramparts were unmarked by the assaults against them. The old fortress, with the glitter of the sea behind it, was dark and still formidable: the scars on its walls too far away to see, only a few jagged gaps in the breastwork around its summit where parts had been broken away to fall on the penthouses of the ill-fated mercenaries.

Some of the men looked back at the fortress almost with regret. The ordeals of cold and hunger and perils were forgotten now. They remembered the boisterous evenings in the hall with music and songs: starlit nights on the ramparts and exciting penetrations of the enemy lines to bring back rabbits. They were returning to homes in the town or fishing huts along the seacoast, or small shacks on the farms. Nothing ever happened there to stir the blood and never would in the times to come, but the days of the siege would be remembered.

www.ingramcontent.com/pod-product-compliance
Ingram Content Group UK Ltd.
Pitfield, Milton Keynes, MK11 3LW, UK
UKHW040640280225
455688UK00002B/24